M. Jennie Kutz

Wab-ah-see

a legend of the Sleeping Dew - and other poems

M. Jennie Kutz

Wab-ah-see
a legend of the Sleeping Dew - and other poems

ISBN/EAN: 9783337391577

Printed in Europe, USA, Canada, Australia, Japan

Cover: Foto ©Andreas Hilbeck / pixelio.de

More available books at **www.hansebooks.com**

WAB-AH-SEE,

—A—

LEGEND OF THE SLEEPING DEW;

AND

OTHER POEMS.

BY

MRS. M. J. KUTZ.

PUBLISHED FOR THE AUTHOR.

CHICAGO:
S. S. BOYDEN, PUBLISHER.
1868.

PREFACE.

—o—

This collection of poems is mainly designed for the numerous friends of the author, with whom she has lived and labored, and who are well acquainted with the principles, motives, and scenes which led to their production. To such, no prefatory remarks are necessary; but, to the stranger, allow me to say, that we recognize eternity as the *birthright* of the human soul, while *time* is the gift of God, upon whose onmoving waves we rear the superstructure of self-preservation—an instinctive impulse in the infant; manifesting itself in the grown man and woman by acts calculated to secure a remembrance when death shall have closed this earthly scene. To this end I have labored, recognizing perfection as the aim of all human aspiration, and happiness as the reward of a well ordered and harmonious life. That eternal justice squares our every word and act; that policy, the antagonist of eternal justice, is the coward's rope, inevitably leading its devotees into inextricable confusion and sorrow; that truth sheds a lasting radiance over all, while falsehood fearfully blackens the falsifier; that duty stands ever before us, demanding the unflinching performance of disagreeable as well as agreeable tasks; that wrong can never become right, and right is right *eternally;* and there cometh a time when the world of men shall recognize these principles. Should this work help to usher in that time, I shall feel that I have not lived or labored in vain.

M. J. K.

Bostwick Lake, Mich., *November*, 1867.

———◆•◆———

CONTENTS.

—o—

WAB-AH-SEE;

A LEGEND OF THE SLEEPING DEW.

THE LONE PINE.

Bright Bostwick! by thy waves I stand,
Where towered once a pine tree grand;
But, at my feet, 'tis lying now,
With shattered trunk and withered bough.
   I lay my hand caressingly
Upon the remnant of the tree,
For, oh! it was a much-prized friend,
That thus hath met untimely end.
   Long years ago, o'er Bostwick's tide,
I saw thee waving in thy pride.
I sat beneath thy breezy shade,
In years that to the past have strayed,
And listened to thy thousand leaves,
That answered to the whisp'ring breeze.
I heard the low-toned waves that break,
Upon the white shores of the lake;
And, to my fancy, all that band
Of waves that knelt upon the strand,

Were vestal virgins of the deep,
In adoration, at thy feet;
Pouring their alabaster store
Of gleaming foam, along the shore.
 And upper deeps, in minstrelsy,
Paid homage to the old pine tree;
For myriads of warblers came
To pour their matins to thy name.
And e'en the sun, in western sky,
Pausing, to bid the world good bye,
Sent back his golden rays to thee—
Grand tribute to thy majesty!
How many times, when twilight came,
And all the west seemed distant flame,
Thy lofty brow hath caught the glow,
Though deepening shadows crept below;
And lighted, like cathedral dim,
Thy leaves made vespers with the wind.
 And how I, too, have loved to stand, .
And worship at thy altar grand,
Admiring all thy circling might,
Thy rugged roots and towering height,
As many, many feet on high,
Thy cone-crowned head rose to the sky.
Thy arms, wide spread on either hand,
As thou wert blessing all the land!
 And when the storm-king swept the lake,
'Till all its waves in white foam break,

How I have raised my arms on high,
To see thee sweep the stormy sky;
And shouting in wild maddening glee,
Encored thy song, thou lone pine tree!
But now, that dream of power is o'er,
For thou art prone upon the shore.
The wind's wild cohorts ye might scorn,
And fling them back upon the storm;
But the fierce thunderbolt's rude jar
Hath scattered thy rude trunk afar;
Hath struck an unresisted blow,
And laid thy year-worn honors low.

Farewell, old pine tree by the lake;
A mournful dirge my numbers wake;
For, ah! this is the last of thee,
Thou had'st no legend history.

And thou, bright lake amidst the wild,
To fame thou art an unknown child.
Thou hast not found a poet's hand
To set in rhyme thy circling strand;
Or, of thy crowning hill tops rave,
That bend around thy southern wave.
Nor lives in song, that child* of thine,
That scarce the midday sun can find,
So deep amid the hills it lies,
It takes the sportsman by surprise.

* A small lake in the hills, much lower than Bostwick, separated
from it by the road, and sometimes connected with it in high water.

A Scott and Burns have sung of Lochs,
Jagged and torn, amid the rocks;
Or flowing streams their pens have bound
In rhyme, and made them " classic ground."
But thy bright waves may sleep for years,
Ye have no tale to charm men's ears.

WAH-NE-GAH.

While thus I sang, with troubled brow,
Of lakelet's wave, and blighted bough,
Lo ! as evoked by my sad tone,
A youth stood on the beach alone.
His dark eye wandered o'er the wave,
As 't were a dearly loved one's grave;
And flashed upon the farther shore,
As if to charm some wanderer o'er.
  My gaze was fixed upon his face,—
He was not of the white man's race.
  His deep round chest, and light free limb,
His eagle eye, and tawny skin,
Told me he was the forest's child,
A warrior hunter, free and wild..
  Long, long he gazed on lake and shore,
And scanned the circling country o'er,
Then, with a savage " ugh " and stare,
He deigned to see that I was there.

I almost seem to see him now,—
His lifted cheek and sloping brow,
His raven hair, and straight lithe form,
His deep set eye (a sleeping storm).
And then his strange apparel too,—
His deer skin leggings fringed with blue;
His hunter's shirt, of fiery red,
Broidered with pure white silken thread.
And then his deerskin mantle, lined
With silver-tinted mohair fine,
Was worn with an exceeding grace,
As one hand held it in its place.
His raven hair flowed down his neck,
A silver band held it in check;
And deftly in that band was set,
The white swan's feather's, held in jet.
I'm sure the hand was small and neat
That wove the covering for his feet;
I've seen them beautiful before,
But not *like* moccasons he wore.

Stretching his free right arm abroad,
He looked fair Nature's sovereign lord.
And pointing to the sleeping lake,
Slowly at first, the strange youth spake;
Then, like the whirlwind rushing past,
His burning words came thick and fast:
 " White squaw laments that none e'er knew
A legend of the Sleeping Dew*;

* Bostwick Lake.

And mourns that shattered old pine tree,
Because it has no history.
Does pale face think this country hath
No moons except for white man's path?   .
Does pale face think that love or fear
Came not where red men chased the deer?
Does pale face know that our big braves
Oft' slept beside these gleaming waves?
Or that tradition makes this tree
A land-mark in our destiny?
If pale face squaw would like to hear,
Wahnegah speak it in her ear.
        Yonder," he pointed to the west,
"Another bright lake spreads its breast;
A mile it is in white man's talk,
The Indian calls it but a walk.
        This one we call the Sleeping Dew,
A name significant to you;
And that we call the Dew Drop's Bride*,
Because they feed each other's tide."
And then he pointed to the north,
" Yonder," he said, " the trail went forth.
A little way it branched in three,
The west led to the Bended Knee;†
The east to Pocamah's‡ low strand,
The middle trail led up the land,

* Silver Lake, or Provin's Lake.   † Beers' or Hayns' Lake.
‡ Cranberry Lake.

Some five quick walks to Wab-ah-see,
Past Deadman's Lake*, to Wampanee."†
Then to the South his fingers swept,
" Close to the lake the trail path crept,
Till at the hills in two it breaks,
That keeping westward past the lakes,
Meets the Gathering Waters trail,‡
Near what the Indian calls Big Wail.§
The plough has spoiled the trail we walked
To hear our old men hold ' big talk,'
You scarce can find where sleep our braves,
The white man's corn above them waves.

The southern trail, 'mid lakes around,
Led to the Big Tree‖ planting ground,

---

* A small lake in Oakfield, lying upon the old trail from Flat River to Plainfield, and the highway for the early settlers as well as for the Indians, and on this lake one of them lost his life. In trying to make his way from Flat River to his brother's house (David Gilbert, still residing in Oakfield,) through the deep snow, he became exhausted, as is supposed, and, sitting down to rest, the death-sleep stole him away to his eternal home. An Indian found him thus, and, without approaching him, walked many times around him to make sure he was dead, then returned to the settlement to call white men to care for their frozen brother. The Indians call all water "bish," peculiarities alone giving distinctive names to any; and, from the sad incident above narrated, this lake received its peculiar appellation.

† Flat River, a belt of Wampum.   ‡ Grand River.

§ Plainfield.   ‖ Ada.

'Where Singing Waters* went to rest
Within the Gathering Waters' breast,
And a huge elm its branches spread,
Above the land that gave us bread.

There fearlessly the song birds came,
And praised the great Manitou's name;
There antlered buck and graceful fawn
Cropped the soft grass at early dawn.
And many wigwams' curling smoke,
The peaceful life of red men spoke.

Oh! how we loved to wander then,
Along the shore, where maples bend,
Beneath the shimmering leaves to glide,
In light canoe, adown the tide.

How loved the spot, where children played
Beneath the swaying elm tree's shade,
Where dark-eyed maids looked fondly out,
And smiled to hear the welcome shout
Of fav'rite hunters, from the chase,
Nearing their sylvan dwelling place.

But, ah! how changed the scene to-day!
The Indian wigwam gone away.
The bounding doe and graceful fawn,
Scared by the white man, too, are gone.
And gone the music of the stream,
Crushed harshly out, like red man's dream!

* Thornapple.

The white man chained the gleaming tide,
And so the Singing Waters died."
  He paused.   I saw his strong chest heave,
Like little child's, when it doth grieve;
And his thin lips, so firmly pressed,
Told me the anguish of his breast.
I thought his eye had gathered tears,
In memory of those other years,
As, backward to the scenes he knew,
His thoughts on noiseless pinions flew.

The White Man's Home.

A statue, motionless as stone,
Long, long he mused on things by-gone,
Then, with a wild, impulsive start,
Forth broke the red man's vengeful heart.
  "Pale face, the white man rears his home
Where once the red man used to roam,
His sharp axe lays the forest low,
Where red men chased the bounding doe.
The white man grinds his corn to-day
Where the free waters used to play.
And all these lands he stole from us,
And scattered us, like clouds of dust.

But, first, he gave us ' drink' that stole
The light from out the red man's soul,
Made ' squaws' of all our biggest braves,
Then robbed us of our fathers' graves!
   Our council fires in blood he quenched;
The white man's plough our graves has trench'd.
His foot treads scornfully the place
Where sleep the buried of our race;
And to the west my people turn,
With saddened hearts, that vengeful burn;
And, where the far-off prairies sweep,
The remnants of our tribes must sleep;—
But, ere the last ' great brave' shall die,
Huge fires shall light the western sky!
   Does pale face think their flames are fed
By autumn grasses, sere and dead?
Wah-ne-gah thinks 'tis Indian ire
Hath set the white man's home on fire,
To light the pale face soul along
The ' death trail' Indian sent it on!"
   He paused again, his eye grew bright,
Then darkened as in sudden night.
   "No good," he said, "No good. 'T will bring
War Eagle down with swooping wing.
Manitou calls for all our braves,
To council fires, beyond our graves.
Wah-ne-gah knew their destiny,
'T was shown him here, beneath this tree."

Eastward he pointed with his hand,—
" Yonder the war-trail crossed the land.
And, when the brave Tecumseh tried
To stay the white man's sweeping tide,
He came upon the Blended Trail,
With Pottawatomies to wail.
But 't was the ' death trail ' for his feet,
When he went forth his ' braves ' to meet;
And, when the great Tecumseh fell,
Hope bade the Indian's heart farewell.

Tecumseh heard, beneath this tree,
He was the red man's destiny :
If *his* should be the victor's hand,
His people should possess the land.
Death or victory for the brave ;
Dominion, or a warrior's grave !
Manitou to the pine leaves sang,
That night, above the ' war dance's ' clang.

Thus to the strife the ' brave ' went out,
And died amidst the battle's shout ;
And back our saddened warriors came,
With nothing but Tecumseh's name.

THE BLIGHTED BOUGH.

" But pale face squaw would like to know
The legend of the blighted bough.

Oh! many, many moons agone,
Before Wah-ne-gah saw the dawn,
A mighty chief, by Wabash' stream,
Beheld this lake side in a dream,
Saw that our scattered tribe would find
Manitou at the lonely pine.
A chief should dwell beside the lake,
To hear what the 'Great Spirit' spake,
That red man's feet might never fail,
On hunter's or the warrior's trail.
And big chief dreamed—in future time
A wanderer, from a far-off clime,
Would seek protection of our tribe;
And that the spirit-voice would chide.
But, heedless of Manitou's voice,
The red man gave the stranger choice;
And, by his serpent trail beguiled,
Would come their downfall, through his child.
The white man's shadow wrapped the tribe,
'Till, one by one, their big chiefs died,
And none were left to point the place
Where sleep the buried of the race.—
The sleeper woke to tell his dream,
By far-off Wabash' rolling stream,
And, led by big chief's prophet eye,
My people left the sunny sky,
And, in this land of lakes and streams,
Fulfilled the "medicine" of dreams.

Great many moons we dwelt beside
These many lakes and river-tide,
'Till, through the wood or on the shore,
Our gray-haired prophet walked no more.
Then pale-face stranger placed his foot
Within the lodge of Monitok,
And asked to be a 'chief' and 'brave,'
He was no coward or a slave.
With haughty step, and peerless grace,
He sought midst warriors for a place,
Nor sought in vain,—the sequel told,
Fulfilling the tradition old.—
A brave he was, so pale and fair,
With golden light along his hair,
And stealthy step, as light and free
As forest hunter's erst might be.

That night Manitou wandered long
Amid the pine leaves' solemn song,
Bidding Wah-ne-gah speak to save
His people from the stranger brave.

The Phantom Boat.

"Three lodges stood beside the lake,
First, Monitok's, the Racer Snake;
Next was the war chief's, Eagle Eye;
Then Big Owl's tent was pitched hard by.

Along the main trail, up the land,
Were camped a numerous warrior band;
Sleeping, to dream the morrow's dawn
Would bring them feasting, joy, and song.
 None but Wah-ne-gah heard the tone
That to the pine tree made its moan;
But when the moon, low in the west,
Laid 'wampum' o'er the bright lake's breast,
And, mantled with a misty sheen,
Its farther shore could not be seen,
A phantom boat, with statued form,
Dark as the spirit of the storm,
Came on the moonbeam's belt of gold,
Straight to the pine tree, lone and old,
And, rising to its utmost height,
Wrapped the green tree in darkest night.
(Wah-ne-gah saw the strange weird thing,
A phantom bird, with sable wing.)
And then, a loud, unearthly wail,
Rang out along the midnight trail,
That roused each warrior from his sleep,
And brought him, frightened, to his feet.
 Each chieftain sprang to open ground,
But direst darkness wrapped him round;
Filled with a moan of chill despair,
Like spirits wailing through the air,
Nor voice, nor darkness left the pine,
'Till the full mid-day sun did shine.

Then to the council fire they came,
Hunters and braves of every name,
And, seated round the old and wise,
Each warrior smoked, with downcast eyes.

At length the chief, Monitok, rose,
And said, 'Warriors of the Long Bows,—
A stranger asks an Indian wife,
A hatchet, belt, and scalping knife,
The white swan's feathers for his hair,
The eagle's claws to bind them there;
A right to hunt our bear and deer,
War paint to make our foemen fear.
Let Big Owl speak up in his place,
Make Indian chief of young pale face?'

Thus summoned, the old chief replied,
'Monitok, bravest of the tribe,
Fleetest of foot, upon the trails,
Compared with thee, old men are snails.'

Then, pointing to his hair, he said—
'Great many snows make white this head;
This wisdom Big Owl has to tell,
Let young chief do his duty well.

This stranger asks a hunter's gear;
Good,—let him chase the bear and deer.
This stranger asks a trader's belt;
Good,—let him take the grey wolf's pelt.
This stranger asks the eagle's claws;
The right to give our young men laws;

Let pale face bring the eagle down,
And bind his talons on his crown,
Then Big Owl give the wise man's place,
In welcome, to the young pale face.
    This stranger asks the big chief's crown,
The white swan's wing, of regal down;—
Upon our trails let white man dwell,
Great many moons, then Big Owl tell.'
    And then the old chief sought his place,
With solemn dignity and grace.
    Great many wise men raised their voice,
And all would give the stranger choice,
'Till Eagle Eye, a youthful brave,
His ' calumet' of friendship waved,
Then spoke,—' Great chieftain, Monitok,
May all your warriors prove a rock,
Unyielding in the battle's might,
Should " Long Knives" come to give us fight;
May all our big braves use their ears,
And keep their hearts from foolish fears;
And, like the Big Owl's, may their eyes,
See when no light is in the skies;
And may their war-cry, wild and free,
Sound fierce as eagle's scream may be,
When soaring to a lofty height,
He rends his prey beyond our sight.
    If pale face wish with us to dwell,
Good,—Eagle Eye will love him well.

But Eagle Eye sees *red* braves here,
Who *fight*, as well as chase the deer.
Would chiefs make stranger pale face free,
What our own braves may never be?
Who tried the stranger brave, to know
His hand draws not a crooked bow?
Who knows his hatchet falls not where
The Indian's midnight lodges are?
First let him in our wigwams dwell
Great many moons, that we may tell
If pale face's heart is truly red.
Monitok, Eagle Eye hath said.'
   Then to his feet Wah-ne-gah sprang,
And through the woods his clear voice rang.
   'Warriors,' he said, 'we own this land,
Made for us by Manitou's hand;
Through forest depths we chase the deer,
And walk these paths without a fear;
Our green corn waves by each bright stream,
And neath these shades our maidens dream;
None come to stay our light fleet tread,
Or fill our hearts with boding dread;
But, should we take this stranger in,
I see along the future, dim,
Disgrace and ruin for our race;—
This land the white man's resting place.
I 've heard that old chief Wake-the-Day,
Dreamed it great many moons away;

And more, Manitou, last dark night,
Spoke out, and gave each warrior fright.
   Last night Manitou gave me dreams;
May be, pale face tell what it means:
   Wah-ne-gah dreamed a big canoe
Took him across a nether blue;
Big waters all around him spread,
As bends the sky above his head.
   Wah-ne-gah saw a regal land,*
Ruled by one big chief's single hand,
And in that land a maiden dwelt,
Who wears this pale face's marriage belt.
What made him leave his blue-eyed bride?
His big chief sent him from her side.
Shall Indian mend a broken bow?
Monitok, bid the pale face go.'
And, with defiant scorn and pain,
Wah-ne-gah sought his place again.

THE ADOPTED BRAVE.

The council rose, the vote they gave,
Made him, not chieftain, but a brave.
And moccasons, a splendid pair,
Wrought by Naontah's fingers fair,
Monitok brought, and laid them down,
Before the stranger, on the ground.

        * France.

A belt of wampum, and a gun,
Laid by them, and the work was done.
With scalp-lock lifted to its place,
And dark paint laid upon his face;—
The stranger stood, a brother brave,
Beneath the pine tree by the wave.
All but Wah-ne-gah joined the smoke,
And loud each warrior's cheer-cry broke,
As round the big chief's lodge they passed,
To see the pale youth, Indian dressed.
Naontah, maid with starry eyes,
Gazed on the stranger with surprise.
Naontah loved the young pale face
More than the warriors of her race.
Her quick ear learned to know his feet,
Her maiden smile grew soft and sweet;
And her soft fingers often stole
Along his curls of jet and gold.
Rare music to her soul, his voice,
Making her inmost heart rejoice.
And so one time, when dew drops bright,
Gleamed in the early morning light,
Monitok missed his daughter's face,
She was not in her customed place.
At middle night, where we stand now,
She sought the pine tree's sheltering bough,
Where wooing lovers, 'neath the light
Of the pure stars, their troth vows plight;

And forth, upon her marriage trail,
She wandered with the stranger pale,
Nor came again, to dwell beside
The chief Monitok, ere he died.
    Long years before, Monitok's bride
Had crossed the sullen river's tide,
And joined the soul's strange shadow band,
That journey to the spirit land.
So none were left Monitok now,
Save Wah-ne-gah, the Blighted Bough.

White Fawn.

    Yonder, the Dew Drop's waves beside,
Dwelt Wah-ne-gah's intended bride.
Wah-ne-gah loved his sister's eyes,
Their starry look of sweet surprise;
But red man's language fails to tell
How White Fawn made his bosom swell.
    Her clear round eyes grew into light,
As stars gleam out along the night;
And graceful as the willow bough,
The silken braids flowed from her brow.
Her pure young face was like the morn,
Or like the full moon, eastward born,
It gleamed along Wah-ne-gah's way,
And turned dark night to brightest day.

Her voice was like the cheery song,
Of soaring lark, at early dawn;
Or, like the mocking bird's, her trill
Stole each glad strain, by glade or rill,
As, free from care, her girlish song
Rang through the forest shades along.
And, when her feet sped on the path,
They made the stones with gladness laugh.
But pale face stranger stole away
The light from Wah-ne-gah one day.
If white squaw listen, she shall know
Why Wah-ne-gah's a blighted bough:

NAONTAH.

Naontah's wigwam stood along,
Where Gathering Waters* sing quick song.
Great many pale face dwell now where
Her wigwam smoke rose on the air;
And where her bark canoe was tied,
In which she crossed the rushing tide,
White man has spanned the broad stream o'er,
With wigwam roof, from shore to shore.†
When twelve young moons looked in the stream,
And twelve old moons paled like a dream,

---

* Grand Rapids.   † Pearl Street Bridge.

Since, from the lodge of Monitok,
Pale face the star-eyed maiden took,
Naontah clasped her bright-eyed boy,
And bade Wah-ne-gah give her joy.
The stranger was not by the stream;
Wah-ne-gah knew his soul was mean;
But Star-Eye* bade him seek the place
Where lingered long the loved pale face,
And bring him to Naontah's side,
To feel a father's worthy pride.
But none could tell where pale face stayed,
And with him, too, the White Fawn strayed;
And when Naontah knew the tale,
Her broken heart made silent wail,
And never more her weary feet
Went forth, the grass and flowers to meet;
But Wah-ne-gah and Monitok
Upon the dying maiden looked,
When, with faltering, feeble breath,
Naontah sang the 'Song of Death.'

Naontah's Death Song.

'Great Maniton, Naontah dies,
Her soul must journey where the skies
Bend downward to the earth's green breast,
Great many moons towards the west.

* Naontah

Naontah knows the trail is bad,
And, oh! her broken heart is sad;
But, with hands clasped upon her breast,
Naontah seeks the land of rest.

Naontah's weary feet must pass
Through the enchanted region vast,
Must seek the "fearful river's" side,
And cross its wildly-rushing tide.

Naontah knows all frightful things,
That move on feet, or flit on wings,
Will meet her on the narrow trail,
But Star Eye's heart must never fail.

With eyes fixed on the farther shore,
Although her feet are worn and sore,
Safely the fearful stream she'll cross;
Naontah's soul must not be lost.'

And then, her voice grown clear and strong,
Rang out in a triumphant song,
That pealed above the rapids' din,
Like victor shouts in battle hymn.

' Naontah knows, when she shall stand
Within the soul's bright " Summer Land,"
The great Manitou will appear,
And wipe away each bitter tear.

Naontah's heart will ache no more,
Upon the river's farther shore;
For loving "shades "* will bathe her feet,
And soothe her with caresses sweet.

And lead her to a lodge most rare,
Where gentle hands shall braid her hair;
And never more her feet will fail,
Upon the flower-decked spirit trail.

No false face make her glad heart break,
Or from her eyes the starlight take;
Great truth alone is ever found,
Within the "Happy Hunting Ground."'

———

And then her words, grown indistinct,
Or wide astray, could not be linked,
But flowed, a wild and tearful wail,
'Till cheek and lip grew cold and pale.
The big chief's heart with grief was bowed,
But *vengeance* young Wah-ne-gah vowed,
As, wrapped in skin of fawn and doe,
They laid her in the ' death canoe,'
And placed her in the earth's dark breast,
Alone, in silent peace to rest.

———

When white man's heart is sore distressed,
Tears ease the anguish of his breast;

* Spirits.

But Indian brave must never know
The blessed teardrop's soothing flow.
A squaw may let her sad heart break,
But warrior's heart must only *hate*;
So Wah-ne-gah, bereft and lone,
Not e'en to waves must make his moan;
But, on his face must lay black paint,
And, though his heart is sore and faint,
Must tie the scalp-lock of his hair,
And, like the grey wolf from his lair,
Go on the trail with noiseless tread,
To strike the treacherous pale face dead.
But, though Wah-ne-gah held his breath,
And his light step was still as death,
The White Fawn's brother, Eagle Eye,
Saw him, and bade the stranger fly.
' No, never !' spake the pale faced brave ;
' Never, if here I make my grave.
Let White Fawn's brother raise his hand,
And, with his own great warrior band,
Sweep Monitok's last brave away !
Let Eagle Eye be chief to-day.'

So, lured by white man's forked tongue,
The war dance and the song were sung;
And braves, who had been friends till late,
Armed for the strive with deadly hate !

At early dawn the war-cry broke
Upon the ears of Monitok,

Whose camp fires burned beside the trail,
Where Indian warriors fell like hail.
Five mounds* upon the spreading plain
Tell of as many big chiefs slain,—
Who sit amid their silent braves,
Within those hugely-swelling graves.

White squaw has read how brave men strike,
Who for a noble purpose fight;
And when with that a great wrong stings,
Men stand like rocks, or fly on wings;
To strike the scoffing foeman's breast,
Or with sharp hatchet cleave his crest.

A BATTLE SCENE.

Not all the hosts of Eagle Eye
Could make Monitok's brave men fly;
But the great chief, Catabanah,
Fell by the knife of Wah-ne-gah;
And the young chieftain, Eagle Eye,
By Monitok's own hand did die.
Two other chiefs, of lesser power,
Fell in that same wild vengeful hour;
At last Monitok laid him down,
With glazing eye, upon the ground.

*. Plainfield.

Wah-ne-gah saw him when he fell,
And, with a wild, terrific yell,
Sprang on the foemen in his path,
Resistless as the whirlwind's wrath,
And for each wound his father bore,
Ten braves went down to sleep in gore.
Oh! fearful was that day of blood,
Beside the Gathering Waters' flood,
Where hundreds of brave warriors slain,
Lay weltering on the battle plain;
But Wah-ne-gah regardless sped
Through living and above the dead,
Straight to the spot where Pale Face tried,
To stay the battle's adverse tide,
With one fierce yell, and mighty bound,
Wah-ne-gah brought him to the ground,
Disarmed him of his keen-edged knife,
And made the Pale Face beg for life;
Backward to his own ranks he pressed,
With Pale Face held before his breast;
Then, with a wild, despairing cry,
Fled every brave of Eagle Eye!
And Wah-ne-gah's brave warriors stood
Triumphant, on the field of blood.
  Twilight was deepening on the plain
When warriors gathered up the slain,
And built huge fires around the dead,
To stay the wild beasts' prowling tread.

Next day, and next, they heaved the mounds,
That mark the Big Wail Planting Grounds;
And white squaw may be sure the name,
Before the awful truth, seems tame.

Then Wah-ne-gah the pale-face took,
Back to the lodge of Monitok;
For Big Owl thought 't was meet that he
Should die beneath the lone pine tree,
Where first his shadow hid the light
Along Wah-ne-gah's pathway bright.

Big Owl bade pale face chant the song
Of death, to cheer his feet along
The strange and unaccustomed way
That leads to whiteman's spirit day;
For never more those feet would tread
The paths that through green forests led.

THE PALE FACE DIES.

The hour had come when vengeance's hand
Would stretch him lifeless on the sand.
Then Pale Face clasped his hands and knelt
Upon the white sand's gleaming belt;
But Wah-ne-gah could never tell
The chant that from his false tongue fell.
Wah-ne-gah's heart laughed out to see
The Pale Face on his bended knee.

Then Big Owl brought Naontah's child,
That sweetly on the Pale Face smiled;
But oh! his eye was hard and stern,
As he, in loathing, from it turned.
And, when his song of death was o'er,
Erect he stood upon the shore;
Haughty and firm the stranger stood,
Gazing on sky, and wave, and wood,
With lofty brow, serene and white,
And, in his eye, a calm, brave light;
To make him kneel Wah-ne-gah tried,
But, firmly standing, white man died!
Red men respect a foeman brave,
But scorn a cringing, coward slave.
Whitemen erect the gleaming stone,
Within their graveyards, weird and lone,
In memory of the good or brave
That sleep beneath the silent grave;
But in Wah-ne-gah's *heart* there stands,
A tablet reared by unseen hands,
Sacred, forever, to the brave,
That fearless fell beside the wave."
Then pointing to a little mound
That marred the sameness of the ground,
" There you will find the Pale Face brave,
We left him kneeling in his grave,
More than a thousand moons ago.
Wah-ne-gah laid the Pale Face low;

But his crushed heart could find no joy,
Not even in Naontah's boy;
Along the woods he joined the chase,
But shadows crept upon his face,
And always to the Sleeping Dew,
Wah-ne-gah's feet Manitou drew.

One night the moon, low in the west,
Laid wampum o'er the bright lake's breast,
Just as it did some moons before,
When Pale Face's feet first sought the shore;
And once again, a light canoe,
Came gliding o'er the Sleeping Dew,
Propelled by one frail maiden's hand,
It grounded lightly on the strand.

Wah-ne-gah watched it in its flight,
Along the moonbeam's belt of light,
And long before the skillful hand
Had brought the frail canoe to land,
Wah-ne-gah's wildly-beating heart,
Told him who steered that fragile bark.

THE WHITE FAWN'S FATE.

Where our lingering feet now stand,
The White Fawn knelt upon the strand,
And, in a low, impassioned wail, '
Her voice took up the mournful tale:

'White Fawn knows well her feet have strayed,
And sad rebuke her heart has made;
But White Fawn was a simple child,
When Pale Face in her wigwam smiled.

List to yon wild bird's frantic cry,
Chained by the serpent's gleaming eye;
It has the *wish* but not the *will*,
To break the charmer's deadly skill;—
And so the poor scared thing must die,
With breaking heart and fearful cry.

But White Fawn, 'neath the stars' pure light,
Has wandered through the solemn night,
To kneel beside the sleeping lake,
And, while her heart cords slowly break,
Beg Wah-ne-gah, for her sad fate,
Only the White Fawn's *faults* to hate.
Just once again she prays to look
Within the lodge of Monitok;
Once more, on the accustomed strand,
Clasp Wah-ne-gah's sustaining hand,
And gaze into his lovelit eye;
Then, peacefully, White Fawn can die.'

But coldly, from the kneeling form,
Wah-ne-gah turned away in scorn;
His heart with love for her was sore,
But still he spurned her from the shore.

Swiftly from land, her light canoe
Sped out upon the Sleeping Dew;

And yonder, where the pale mist creeps,
Beneath its waves the White Fawn sleeps.
  Wah-ne-gah watched her as she went,
But his proud heart would not relent;
Stern fate had swept from him his bride,
Returnless as time's onward tide.
Some time, amid the bowers *above*,
He'd seek again his truant love;
But *she* could ne'er return to *him*,
O'er wrong's broad chasm, deep and dim.
  The sad moon hid her brow of light,
Behind a storm-cloud's breast that night,
And soon a tempest swept the shore,
That every wave in white shreds tore;
But still, erect, beneath the pine,
Wah-ne-gah watched the scene sublime.
And sighed that winds should ever sleep,
Or raindrops should forget to weep,
As, like an army, rushing by,
The storm-cloud sought the eastern sky,
And fitfully, through forests deep,
Sobbing, the tempest went to sleep;
But never more the painful thrill
That crept through heart and brain, until,
Borne onward by death's fateful tide,
Wah-ne-gah's arms should clasp his bride.
  Twice had the moonbeam's belt of light
Been thrown across the lake at night;

And, anchored 'neath the old pine tree,
Twice had it brought sad prophesy.
Wah-ne-gah knew for him, once more,
That belt of light would reach the shore,
And, in some mysterious way,
His feet along its track would stray;
And braves would seek in vain for him,
In paths that led through forests dim.

For years he watched the moon to rest,
Behind the dark woods in the west;
And turned each time, to join the chase,
With deeper shadows on his face.
No wigwam smoke curled on the breeze,
No bright eyes watched beneath the trees,
No sweet voice sang a welcome song,
To cheer his weary feet along;
None clung to him for succor now,—
Wah-ne-gah was a blighted bough.

Wah-ne-gah prayed the lightning's stroke
To cleave him, as it clave the oak;
Or asked the fearful whirlwind's breath
To sweep him to the shades of death;
But prayed in vain; his weary feet
Must *walk* the golden belt to meet.
And, when great many moons had died,
Wah-ne-gah saw it on the tide;
It came at last, that belt of gold,
Along the sleeping waters cold,

While, on Wah-ne-gah's startled car,
A well-known voice rang sweet and clear.

The Song of the White Canoe.

' Monitou bids the White Fawn wake
Wah-ne-gah, by the sleeping lake;
And, with his hand clasped in her own,
Send him upon the death trail lone.

Wah-ne-gah's heart need feel no fear,—
The White Fawn's hand his bark will steer;
Where Monitok and Silver Bough*
Are waiting for Wah-ne-gah now.

For, while the earth is wrapped in sleep,
And pale mists on the waters creep,
The white canoe† glides o'er the wave,
To bear away the sad-eyed brave.

* Wah-ne-gah's mother.

† The Indians believe that those who kill themselves in consequence of trouble, are borne to the spirit land in a white canoe, to ease their journey, in pity for their previous sufferings, while those who die a natural death must reach the spirit land on foot, by a weary journey of many months towards the setting sun, terminated by a fearful river, crossed only by a small slippery log, where all frightful phantoms beset the traveler; and, if he keeps his eyes fixed on the farther shore, he enters the Happy Hunting Grounds, otherwise he is lost forever.

The Blighted Bough no more shall stand
Upon the wave-washed, gleaming strand,
With bare arms reaching o'er the tide,
Waiting to clasp his spirit bride.

The whip-poor-will at dawn shall wake
The echoes by the sleeping lake,
And thousand tones through woodlands thrill
In answer to the whip-poor-will;

But they will break thy dreams no more,
For thou shalt leave the circling shore;
Borne away, o'er a sea of blue,
Crossed alone by the white canoe."

Borne away where the skies are bright,
Where falsehood brings no chilling blight;
And lotus flowers perfume the air,
Drowning for aye the dream of care.'

The sweet voice sang, with pathos rare,
Thrilling along the midnight air;
And then, upon the waves of light,
A vision floated into sight.
Wab-ne-gah knew the sylph-like form,
Lost in the dark night's fearful storm,
When, years before, with scornful hand,
He spurned her, kneeling on the sand.

One farewell look Wah-ne-gah gave
The lone pine by the lakelet's wave;
One parting glance o'er forests dim;
Gazed round the arching heaven's rim;
And then, with swift and eager feet,
Went forth, his spirit bride to meet.
Traditions tell, the way is long,
And fearful shades the trail-path throng,
That leads by earth's far western bounds,
To red man's happy hunting grounds:
But Wah-ne-gah saw none of these,
Beneath the softly whispering trees,
That shade the red man's home beside
The blessed river's crystal tide.
Wah-ne-gah's soul just went to sleep,
And wakened at the White Fawn's feet!

THE MEDICINE SPRING.

White squaw sees yonder, through the wood,
Straight east from where the pine tree stood,
A huge oak lifts its leafy crest,
Above a simple brooklet's breast;
And down the bank, beneath its shade,
A sacred lodge our fathers made.

Your feet have wandered by the stream*
That makes its way like midnight's dream;
Its source hid erst from mortal eyes,
Its fountain in the deep lake lies.

Big Owl, loved chief of all the tribe,
Saw *healing* in the simple tide;
For, when Manitou stirr'd the wave,
Great strength to sick and lame it gave.
Great many 'walks,' from east and west,
Poor Indian came, with pain distressed,
And waited, in the shadows deep,
The coming of Manitou's feet.

The Indian, Nature's simple child,
Dwelling amid the forests wild,
Untrammeled by the white man's lore,
Trusted and loved Manitou's power;
But, long ago, their footsteps strayed
From 'neath the oak tree's sacred shade;
A false life sweeps them to the grave,
Resistless as the ocean wave.

---

* The spring referred to is situated on the farm now owned by Albert Davies; and when the place was taken by his father, the old oak stood there in its majesty, and the table land above the spring was clear of undergrowth, shaded with trees, and carpeted with soft Indian grass. The spring boils furiously at times, as also the bed of the little stream into which it runs. The place was evidently a favorite camping ground for the red men, now gone from it for ever.

And when Big Owl lay down to die,
Manitou bade him prophesy:
'Speak 'gainst my people's straying feet,
Gone out the white man's guile to greet.'

BIG OWL'S PROPHESY.

'Red men, dwelling by every tide,
Stalking through forests deep and wide,
Numerous as the falling leaves,
Stirr'd by the autumn's fitful breeze.
Manitou gave you sinews strong
As buffalo's thrice twisted thong;
With skill to conquer, in the wood,
The wild game made for red man's food.
And here and there, by every stream;
Bright as the spirit of a dream,
Manitou set, in circling hills,
The planting grounds the red man tills;
And, with Manitou's gift of corn,
The red man laughs grim want to scorn,
When deepening snows lie on the plain,
And sounding footsteps scare the game.
For you, Manitou raised the trees,
And laid their green leaves on the breeze,
Spread His blue blanket o'er your head,
And spangled it with golden thread.

Gave summer's sun the power to raise,
From damp, dark clods, the golden maize.
Hung up the silver moon on high
To gather dew drops in the sky,
And scatter them with queenly hand,
As blessings, o'er a parching land,
When storm-clouds send their treasured rain,
To cool the sun god's fevered brain.
Manitou gave you big owl's sight,
Unerring in the darkest night;
And, for the day, the eagle's gaze,
Unflinching in the sun's bright rays.
Manitou gave you feet to speed,
As flits the wild bird o'er the mead.
The long bow in your hand he laid,
The quiver at your shoulder stayed.
And led you by the running stream,
Or where bright lakes 'mid forests gleam;
And gave you all this wide-spread land,
Made for you by His loving hand;
With antlered buck and bounding doe,
The wild bear and the buffalo,
A plenteous chase for red man's feet,
Within the wild wood's cool retreat.
And sweetly, by the babbling streams,
To red man's sleep came pleasant dreams.
Manitou's children numerous grew,
As morning's gleaming drops of dew.

But when the white man's forked tongue,
Big lie in Indian's weak ear sung,
Then red man spurned the gleaming wave,
And strove in " fire " his thirst to lave!
His long bow from his hand he flung,
And took the white man's speaking *gun*,
That, like Manitou's voice of wrath,
Scared all the wild game from his path.
Now Manitou has hid his face,
In darkness, from the red man's race.
Big Owl now sees His vengeful hand,
Stretched out in wrath above this land!
Indian hath scorned Manitou's love,
And now the white man's feet shall shove
The red man's foot from every path;
Manitou speaks it in his wrath.'

    Then Big Owl raised his dying hand,
And pointed to the pine tree grand—
'The lofty brow of yon huge oak,
Shall fall beneath the white man's stroke,
When my poor people's straying feet
Have gone the western wave to meet;
But thou, lone pine, beside the shore,
Shall scorn the white man's puny power!
Manitou loves the pine tree's song,
When red men in its shadows throng;
And it shall stand above the wave,
A land mark to each lingering brave,

'Till the last form shall fade that knew
The legend of the Sleeping Dew;
Then Manitou's own hand will take
The pine tree from the gleaming lake.'

———

Then Big Owl laid his stately head
Upon the green earth's genial bed,
Composed his limbs in quiet rest,
With folded arms across his breast,
And peacefully, as good men die,
Went on his journey to the sky.

THE WHITE SWAN.

When Wah-ne-gah first took the babe
Naontah in his strong arms laid,
The dying sister asked that he
Would call the bright boy Wab-ah-see*;
And ever, for his mother gone,
They called the Pale Face's boy White Swan.
But never once Wah-ne-gah smiled
Upon Naontah's lonely child;
His vengeful heart could not forget
That white blood through those dark veins set,

* White Swan.

Or that such curling rings of hair
The treacherous Pale Face used to wear;
So Wahnegah gave him to one
Who gladly hailed him as his son.
    The spirit of the winter came,
And scattered snow along the plain;
The spring, amid the naked trees,
With breezy fingers wove green leaves;
And summer flung its robe of flowers
Around the golden-tinted hours;
Then autumn walked with solemn tread,
Among the grasses sere and dead;
But all the changing seasons smiled
Upon Naontah's orphan child,
'Till, like the oak, his limbs grown strong,
Bore him with stately tread along,
The way big chief alone may walk,
Called by the council-fire to talk.
    Wah-ne-gah thought Naontah's eyes
Gleamed ever from the starry skies,
And ever, with their holy light,
Guided her boy by day and night.
In no stray paths his feet went by,
He was the light of each brave's eye;
Old warriors blessed him when they died,
And young braves watched his steps with pride.
Big Medicine said, 'Destiny
Smiled on the young chief Wab-ah-see.'

One day the White Swan claimed his bride,
The brightest maiden of the tribe,
And with gay thongs, made up of flowers,
Thrown round the waist of Sunny Hours,
Led her by gleaming Wab-ah-see,
His wigwam's light henceforth to be.
Young children came, and sweetly smiled
Upon Naontah's noble child;
But, all this time, the white man's hands
Were gathering up the red man's lands.
May be, pale face may never know
What feelings in the bosom grow,
When trampling feet tread out the light,
That made the spirit's pathway bright;
May be, pale face has never known
What 't was to wander from her home,
And know her feet would never more
Come back to find the home of yore;
If pale face loves the buds that fling
Their beauty in the lap of spring;
If pale face loves the flowers that grow;
The free wild winds that fitful blow;
If pale face loves the voice of floods,
The solemn murmur of the woods;
If pale face loves the wild birds' song,
Warbled by sunny meads along;
If pale face loves the starry night,
Or crystal dew drops' gleaming light;—

Let pale face close her eyes for aye,
To all the grandeur of the sky;
Forever quench the sun's bright beams,
And hush the murmur of the streams;
See not the glorious earth again,
Save in memory's mournful strain;
And voiceless, sightless, helpless drift
Down some dark chasm's dismal rift,
Then, maybe, pale face's heart can guess,
Somewhat of red man's wild distress,
When, from his helpless hands were rent,
The bright scenes where his youth was spent,
And ruthlessly the plow share crept
O'er green graves, where his fathers slept!
Ashes, by trails, lie cold and deep,   .
Where council fires were wont to leap,
And wearily my people stray,
Fading, like summer clouds, away.
The white man holds, with tightening hands,
These running streams and broad spread lands,
And crowds the red man's lingering form
Nearer the land where sleeps the storm.
The pale face should not wonder if,
Goaded by wrongs, his hands uplift;
Or sometimes, in the dark midnight,
His fearful 'war cry' makes 'big fight."

One day white brother came to call
Our gathered chiefs in council hall,
And asked to buy our streams and woods,
With knives and beads, and useless goods;
Said 'Big *White* Father' loved red skin;
And wished great happiness to him.
And fiery rum, with free hand plied,
For days, by Gathering Waters' tide.
But every brave chief, Indian born,
Turned from the brother's talk with **scorn**,
'Till Wab-ah-see, seduced by gold,
The red man's birthright from him sold.

Wild consternation filled each band
Of warriors, scattered through the land,
When Indian runners, on each trail,
Sped forth, to spread the direful tale,
And of the wise men form a band,
To hunt the traitor through the land.

The Pursuit.

None knew where he had sought to hide,
Along the streams and forests wide;
But, when the red man seeks his foe,
He marks each slight twig bended low;

The trampled blade of grass replies
To his quick-seeing, piercing eyes;
Even a pebble, stirred but slight,
Reveals a human footstep's flight;
The startled cry of owlet heard,
The sudden flitting of a bird,
The passage of a beast of prey,
Flying across the woods by day,
The slightest wreath of curling smoke,
The faintest sound of paddle stroke,
Tells to the red man's listening ear,
The lurking foeman's footsteps near:
    Thus on and on brave Wab-ah-see
Was tracked along the land and lee,
Until, one mellow autumn day,
The traitor chief was brought to bay.
    The wild deer startled in the fell,
By stag hound's bay or hunter's yell,
Will pause not in his rapid flight,
Except upon some friendly height,
Where, sheltered by a leafy screen,
Seeing the foe, himself unseen,
He gathers up his panting breath,
And flies again the hand of death.
Thus Wab-ah-see had paused to rest
Upon the highland's lifted crest.
White squaw great many times has passed
Where Wab-ah-see was caught at last;

In mounds* great many warriors sleep,
Among the seven lakes called Wab-queet.†
  'T was high noonday. Among the trees
A light smoke floated on the breeze;
And just a taint of broiling meat,
The hungsy hunters' nostrils greet;
There, sheltered by a swelling mound,
The chief lay stretched upon the ground.
A cordon of brave warriors crept
Around the big chief, while he slept,
Unheard, behind the hill they meet,
And hem him in, with stealthy feet;
Each warrior, armed with knife and thong,
Slowly but surely crept along.
A moment more, a dozen hands
Would bind the chief in captive bands,
When, lo! a stone, in shallow bed,
Loosened, adown the hill side sped:
Slight sound it made along its route,
But echo caught it with a shout,
And ringing back, from wood and lakes,
The mimic sounds, the warrior wakes.
Confused, and startled by the noise,
He brought his stately form to poise,
And with presented weapons stood,
Peering along the silent wood.

  * Still to be seen on Alonso Bigford's farm, in Oakfield.
       † A flock of quails.

The Capture.

Old hunters know how pulses leap,
What thrills along the muscles creep,
When, just upon the path, the prey,
Hard pressed, is fiercely brought to bay;
But where's the language meet to tell,
What feelings in the bosom swell,
When *Man's* the game that leads the chase;
And *brother* hunts his brother's face?
There stood the chief, with flashing eye,
His muscles tense to fight or fly;
His foot firm planted on the ground,
His head half bent to catch each sound;
His splendid form against the sky,
Outlined upon each warrior's eye,
Whose feelings grew akin to awe,
While gazing on the brave outlaw.
Death stared each warrior in the face
Who dared to leave his hiding place;
And every brave, with crouching form,
Shrank from the bursting of that storm,
That surged, in waves of fearful ire,
Through Wab-ah-see's fierce heart of fire.
Full well they knew his mighty power,
His prowess in the battle hour,
When *his* was like the lightning's stroke,
That cleaves in twain the sturdy oak;

And dying bruin's last caress,
Hugging the hunter to her breast,
Was gentle as the *vengeful* clasp
Of Wab-ah-see in days gone past.
Who dares to meet his anger now,
When dark despair sits on his brow?
  Look! Conistoga, with a thong,
In lasso noose, creeps slow along;
On, on, then, with a tiger bound,
Sends forth the cord, with whizzing sound,
And, when the thong his sure hand flings,
His fearful war-cry fiercely rings.
True to its aim, the thong fell down,
And brought the pinioned chief to ground.
Oh! then the stilly air was rent,
With yells that burst like thunder pent,
'Till sheer exhaustion stayed the clang,
That through the sounding wild woods rang,
As scores of warriors pressed to see
The prostrate form of Wab-ah-see.
And, gloating o'er the big chief's fall,
They dragged him to the council hall,
Where thronging chiefs and warriors came,
With boding eyes, and hearts aflame,
Eager to seal their deathless hate,
With blood of one revered so late.
  Just as the awful hush that falls
Upon the earth, the heart appalls,

When, surging up the western sky,
A fearful storm cloud meets the eye;
Just as we know its shadows deep,
But hide the tempest's trampling feet,
So Wab-ah-see was well aware,
That vengeance moved each dusk form there,
Though every warrior took his place
With no emotion on his face;
Knew it before Cogmosa grim,
Laid black paint on his tawny skin,
And turned him in the big chief's place,
To show the death vote on his face.

THE REPRIEVE.

No word the sullen warriors speak,
As each one stains his dusky cheek,
Until Conote, the Red Chief, stood,
And asked to stay the vote of blood.

  ' Where is the purchase for our lands?
The gold is in the White Swan's hands.
Where shall we seek it when he sleeps,
And forth his guilty spirit creeps?
Warriors, forbear the vote of death,
And let us grant our brother breath.

May be, some day he'll give the gold
For which our hunting grounds were sold.'
  So he was banished to the shore,
Where waves gleamed at his wigwam door;
One walk beyond the bright lake's breast,
From north to south, from east to west.
The trees were 'blazed' to mark the grounds,
If Wab-ah-see strayed past those bounds,
Then every brave might raise his hand,
And blot the White Swan from the land.
  All artifice was tried, in vain,
To draw from him his ill-got gain.
Sometimes 't is Sunny Hours pleads,
Anon, his daughters ask for beads;
And then his son would go to school;
But Wab-ah-see was 'no big fool.'
None ever saw the white man's gold,
For which the hunting grounds were sold.
  Great many warriors slept and ate,
With Wab-ah-see beside the lake,
When snows lay deep along the wood,
Where White Swan's many lodges stood.
Great many times, when summer's sheen
Wrapped all the earth in deepest green,
Pursued the bounding deer with him,
O'er sunny slopes, through valleys dim,
But never once, in heat of chase,
Did he forget to note the place,

And never once his footsteps strayed
Past land marks by the council made.
But time sped onward down the years,
And took from him distrust and fears.
Warriors whose feet were free to roam,
Saw, gathering still, the white man come;
But Wab-ah-see, beside the shore,
Saw not the white man's crushing power;
Knew not, with every moon's return,
Fiercer each savage bosom burned,
As maddened by the growing throng,
Each warrior nursed his deadly wrong,
'Till, wakened by the white man's feet,
Swift Vengeance would no longer sleep.

WAB-AH-SEE BETRAYED.

The green corn waved its tasseled head,
On plains where slept our slaughtered dead,
And where our council lodge then stood,
Beside the mighty river's flood,
Our gathered bands were wont for days
To hold the feast of the green maize.
Then maddened braves, with many lies,
And oft averted, crooked eyes,
Begged of the once beloved chief
From banishment to seek relief;

Urged him, for sake of his old braves,
To feast beside the rushing waves,
And with the merry dance and song,
Help speed the lagging hours along.
But grim Distrust sat in the door,
And spurned the tempters from the shore,
'Till by-gone hours, a ghostly band,
Assailed the chief on every hand,
And thronging memories rushed to tell,
How, once, his warriors loved him well,
While maidens bright their offering flung,
And praises of his great deeds sung.
' Oh ! might not love have conquered hate,
And honors in his pathway wait?'
'T was thus Ambition's syren tongue,
Insidious, to his weak heart sung,
'Till grim Distrust fled from her post,
And Wab-ah-see, the chief, was lost.

May be, the white squaw's cheek would pale,
If Wah-ne-gah should tell the tale;
And may be, too, her heart would ache,
For Wab-ah-see, of yon bright lake,
Who, straying from its sunny shore,
Would never see its bright waves more.
May be, her heart would scorn the lie
That lured the traitor chief to die.
May be, white squaw would hail *him* lord,
Who stood among that howling horde,

With folded arms across his breast,
Defiant eye and lifted crest;
And dauntless, 'mid the savage clang,
His brave deeds in a death song sang.
May be, pale face would love that soul,
That dared the taunt of 'hidden gold;'
And brought the murderous weapon down,
That stretched him bleeding on the ground.
White Swan knew well that never more
His feet would press yon sunny shore;
Or follow more, in winding trace,
The glad streams in their rapid race;
That never more the sun, for him,
Would light the arching heaven's rim;
Or stars smile downward in his face,
From their far-distant homes in space.
White Swan knew well a heart of fire
Lit up each baleful face with ire,
And, scorning them, with lofty pride,
Like a true warrior, White Swan died.
But hate pursued him when he fell,
And louder grew each savage yell,
Till Reason, reft of her control,
Far from the frantic conclave stole;
Until the deepening shades of night
Took from the stream its glinting light;
And, palsied by excess, red braves,
Prone senseless, slept beside the waves.

White squaw need never lift her form,
And curl her lip in bitter scorn;
Wah-ne-gah knows that white man's drink,
Has power the bravest soul to sink.
If Wah-ne-gah were white man's God,
He'd surely lift the vengeful rod,
And strike that vile miscreant dumb,
Who dared to tempt with fiery rum!

But, from that night of shameful sleep,
Slowly, at last, the shadows creep;
Slowly the beaming morning came,
With flashing wheels of golden flame,
That reached and roused the stulted brain
Of redmen, sleeping on the plain,
And, slowly, recollection told,
That Wab-ah-see was stark and cold.

THE BURIAL OF WAB-AH-SEE.

Oh! pitiless the hand to slay,
Relentless still, to lure its prey.
But when his voice in death was still,
Memories thronged the heart to thrill;
And many feet, with silent tread,
Moved slow, in honor of the dead.

In regal state the chief was laid,
With death dance, to appease his shade;*
But none forgot, for white man's gold,
Their pleasant hunting grounds he sold.
But, when the dark night shadows came,
With many torchlights' glaring flame,
They bore the big chief to his rest,
Upon the highland's lifted crest;
They placed him sitting on the hill,†
That he might see the white man till
The broad plains where his fathers sleep,
When gone were all his people's feet;
They placed him sitting in his grave,
Where he could see the gleaming wave,
And watch the white man's big canoe,
When faded were the forms he knew;
They placed him by the white man's trail,
Where he might see the stranger pale,
And where his passing feet should be
A long rebuke to treachery!

---

* The Indians believe that the spirit of the dead clings to earth to wreak its vengeance; and this dance was instituted as an honor to the departed, to appease their wrath in such cases.

† This hill is now well known as " Plainfield Bluffs," and the exact spot where the body rests is familiar to the people all through that region. The remains were visible in their sitting position until about 27 years ago, when they were buried by the whites.

White squaw will wonder how the brave
Could see the white man from his grave.
They roofed his grave with little trees,
And bade him wait and watch through these.
But wofully the red men rued,
The day their hands in blood were brued,
For ever, at the feast of corn,
Was heard his voice of taunting scorn;
And here and there his vengeful soul,
Led on the hunt for hidden gold;
When, in some lone and tangled fell,
Would ring his wild, unearthly yell.
Each new moon, in his grave was laid,
Tobacco, to appease his shade;
But still, the chief who laid him low,
Grew nerveless as an unstrung bow,
And, when the White Swan's drooping head
Told Indian that his soul had sped,
He went not on the death trail lone,
The Red Chief, too, had with him gone!

CONCLUSION.

White squaw, my people's race is run,
Few wander near the setting sun;
Few wait beside the great lake's shore,
The death canoe, to bear them o'er.

Their fate is like this shattered pine,
Broken, yet grand in its decline.

White squaw, some moons ago this tree,
With its broad branches, sheltered thee;
But yonder, rolling up the west,
The fearful storm cloud heaves its breast,
Charged with the lightning's fiery breath,
To strike this old tree to its death!

Look! how the tempest's tramping feet,
Fright the scared waves along the deep,
As, with a broadening sheet of foam,
They near the pine tree old and lone,
That backward heaves each shiv'ring bough,
Like parted waves before the prow.

Fierce sweep the howling winds along,
And wilder grows the pine tree's song,
'Till, from the storm-cloud's sable breast,
A bolt of thunder cleaves its crest;
And, yielding to Manitou's power,
The pine lies shattered on the shore.

DEATH OF COGMOSA.

And all his weary marching done,
Beside the waves of Michigan,
An aged warrior slept to wake,
Where fearful tempests never break.

More than a thousand moons, his feet
Had walked, the flowers of earth to meet;
More than a hundred snows had shed
Their whiteness on Oogmosa's head;
But in the tempest's fearful roar,
That laid this pine tree on the shore,
His spirit joined the shadowy band
That journey to the Happy Land;—
And thus had passed the last who knew
The Legend of the Sleeping Dew!"

POEMS

FOR

FUNERAL OCCASIONS.

POEMS

FUNERAL OCCASIONS.

THE AGED DEAD.

My friends, ye ask of me a strain,
　　Of rhythm slow and sad;
Like mourners moving in the train,
Winding along the solemn plain,
　　Bearing your sacred dead.

I know a patriarch has gone,
　　An aged friend has passed
From scenes in which he mingled long,
A useful member 'mid the throng
　　With whom his lot was cast.

Full well I know an empty chair
　　Awaits your tearful gaze;
And lonely hours are thronging there,
And vacant places everywhere
　　Remind of other days.

Ah ! well your agony I know,
   And feel with you to grieve;
But still my lines refuse to flow
In sympathetic strains of woe;
   A *nobler* verse I weave.

My soul starts up in glad surprise,
   And eager pen leaps on,
To tell the joys that meet my eyes,
Through pearly gate way in the skies,
   Where our loved friend has gone.

Youth stands upon the gleaming shore,
   Beyond the sullen tide,
And waits the boat with muffled oar,
Bearing the aged pilgrim o'er,
   That wandered from your side.

And, with a wonder-working wand,
   Will bid his manhood's might
Enwrap him, like a garment grand,
When he shall reach the shining strand
   Beyond Death's chilling night.

How can I sing a mournful strain,
   While, gazing on that shore,
I hear, above the solemn main,
Or breakers roar, the soul's refrain,
   Life's song, for evermore ?

LAY ME TO REST.

Written for the Funeral of a Lady burned to death.

Lay my form down in the cold, cold ground,
    And leave it to sleep in the dust;
For only the casket the coffin hath bound,
    Neath the clods ye so nicely adjust.

Lay me to rest where rolling plains spread,
    And the forests are waving nigh;
But, mind ye, my soul sleepeth not with the dead;
    That hath sped to its home on high.

Lay my charred frame in the cold, cold ground,
    And weep ye, but not in despair;
For sweetly it sleeps in this low swelling mound,
    Unvexed by affliction or care.

Lay me down here, to sleep in the ground,
    And hallow my grave with a sigh;
But journeying on past the world's weary bounds,
    Come meet me, in mansions on high.

LIFE IN DEATH.

Written for the Funeral of Mrs. Lewis Snyder.

Oh, Man! how beauteous is the life,
  Thy God hath given thee;
Through all the world's wild toil and strife,
  It makes a *god* of thee.

The strange mysterious forms of clay,
  We bury in our graves;
Build up, and bear the soul away,
  To death's baptismal waves.

But while this strange wrought house of clay
  Builds, and bears on the soul,
Hid in Life's corner stone away
  There is a record scroll.

Time's hand the ponderous stone shall raise,
  Exhume the record rare;
And Death will vanish in the blaze
  Of knowledge written there.

We gaze out toward the golden gates
  That fold the sun at even;
Yonder, the sun the morning waits,—
  So life goes up to heaven.

And thus this shattered frame of clay
　Is buried in the earth;
But life keeps on its mystic way,
　The soul through death hath birth.

We fold her toil-worn, weary hands
　Upon her aged breast;
Youth greets her in the Morning Lands
　That shore the Sea of Rest!

Farewell! farewell! thy life bark glides
　Far out upon the sea;
We gaze, but mist our vision hides;
　We wait to follow thee.

Beyond death's billows, angels greet
　Thee, with a joyous shout;
And many *loved* to-day ye meet,
　Who long ago went out.

Sometimes *we* gaze on the shining sands
　Thy risen feet may press;
And catch the gleam of pure white hands,
　That soothe thy soul's distress.

Where in that far-off spirit world,
　Beyond our Central Sun;
Life's gorgeous banners are unfurled,
　When Time's weird march is done.

And, oh! the gathering hosts that stand
   Upon the Hills of Light;
Or move in sweeping columns grand,
   Dispelling Error's night!

Blest soul! I almost long to be,
   An earth-bound child no more;
As, gazing through the mists, I see
   Thy form upon yon shore!

Farewell! farewell! again I say;
   Hushed is thy earthly voice;
But, o'er the Hills of Life away,
   Thy spirit shouts "rejoice!"

THE TRANSLATED.

*Written for the Funeral of Walter M., infant son of T. M.
and L. A. Morse, of Oakfield.*

Little Walter, thou art passing,
   Passing from our sight away;
But an angel band enfolds thee,
   In the realms of endless day.

Thou hast suffered—sadly suffered—
  Suffered more than mortals know;
But the angel Death hath kindly
  Borne thee hence from mortal woe.

Thy hands we have gently folded,
  On thy still and pulseless breast,
Cheered thy little spirit homeward,
  To the land of quiet rest.

Now thy infant feet are pressing,
  Paths that wind mid heavenly bowers,
And thy ears are charmed with music,—
  Music of the Holy Hours.

Birds for thee, of gorgeous plumage,
  Trill sweet notes within those bowers;
Living diamonds gleam and sparkle
  Neath thy feet, amid the flowers.

Angels fold thee to their bosoms,
  By the crystal Sea of Life;
Teach thee God's most holy lessons,
  Free from earthly sin and strife.

And beneath the holy sunlight,
  Of that fairer world than this,
Ye will grow to perfect stature,
  Knowing only *truth* and *bliss*.

Fare-thee-well ! thou little spirit,
 Farewell ! to thy form of clay;
Sometimes come, as our Evangel,
 Bringing news from realms of day.

THE ARISEN.

Written for the Funeral of T. N. Morse, of Oakfield.

The husband is an angel now,
 With robes by death made white;
And crowned, the father's radiant brow,
 Within a land of light.

Last morn he joinéd his hands with those
 Who long ago went o'er;
And from the whirlpool, death, arose,
 Safe on the spirit shore.

He dwells beside the waves that flow
 Near the Eternal throne;
But charms, with gentle hand, the woe
 That makes bereaved ones moan.

His spirit bark he often steers
 To shores he left behind;
And gently wipes the bitter tears
 That sad, sad eyes make blind.

He gathers spirit flowers that grow
  On the Eternal Shore,
And drops them one by one below,
  'Till pain is felt no more.

You *feel* his presence in the air
  That breaks around his home;
He gathers with the loved ones there,
  To still each heart's sad moan.

He cannot sleep within this grave!
  The earthly mound may swell;
But, o'er Death's tide, Life's banners wave!
  Weep not, for " all is well."

THE BOATMAN.

Written for the funeral of Mrs. Abner Wright, of Otisco.

I would sing to you of a dim shore seen,
A phantom boat, and a silent stream;
A muffled oar, and a filling sail,
And of a Boatman, cold and pale.

Our children, whose feet approach that stream,
Fade from us like a fleeting dream;
As, folded close in the Boatman's arms,
They drift away from life's alarms.

Hark! a tiny shout rings down the vale,
When they behold the snowy sail;
Their hands fly up, and their eyes grow bright,
When spirit shores loom on their sight.

Then their eyelids close, and soft hands fold,
Their cheeks turn pale, and lips grow cold;
And evermore we must seek in heaven,
For those whose forms to dust are given.

Our sisters go out with the Boatman pale,
Wafted on by the chilling gale;
And our brothers cross the solemn tide,
Traveling aye by the Boatman's side.

And our souls rise up and ask for the gone;
Hark! o'er the stream we hear their song!
The mist rolls by, and we see them stand,
Conquering palms in every hand!

On the father's brow the death damp stands,
Wrung by the Boatman's unseen hands;
Folding him round with a mantle white,
Wrapping him in from mortal sight.

Friends, wife, and children gathering round,
See a smile, but they hear no sound;
His voice is hushed on the solemn tide,
Drifting him to the other side.

The mother goes out with the Boatman pale,
A snowy robe, and a filling sail;
A panting sigh, and a gurgling sound,
And her voice, too, by the tide is drowned.

While her weeping children are bending low,
Longing across the tide to go;
To nestle upon the loved one's breast,
Ever in sacred peace to rest.

But, ah! they must walk the world's chill gloom,
Wearily on to the silent tomb;
Must learn hard lessons of patient grief,
Waiting the boat for their relief.

But, thanks to God, we know that they,
Gone over the silent stream away,
Are ever watching, where skies are clear,
Over the storms that gather here.

And, with inward eye, we may see them stand,
Robed in white, in the spirit land;
Their fair arms reaching over the tide,
Hailing us from the other side.

There cometh a time when we shall stand,
Listing, the boat anear the strand;
Shall catch the gleam of the phantom sail,
Swelling out on the chilling gale.

Be rowed by him of the muffled oar,
Across the stream, to the farther shore;
Where friends long parted again shall greet,
And throbbing hearts forever meet.

IN THY PRESENCE, DEATH.

*Written for the Funeral of Jay, only son of John and Betsy
Davis, of Oakfield.*

With folded hands and 'bated breath,
I stand within thy presence, Death;
And gaze upon this stricken form,
O'erwhelmed by dissolution's storm.

How still and pulseless lies the heart,
That throb by throb with life did part;
How firm the pale, cold lips are pressed,
How breathless lies the palsied breast.

Chill blow the breezes from yon shore,
Where Boatman pale, with muffled oar,
Launches his bark upon the waves
That roll beside the land of graves.

And chill mists roll round watchers pale,
Waiting to hear the Boatman's hail;
And, oh! despite our prayers and tears,
Away with them the Boatman steers.

Standing with them beside the shore,
 We cannot hear the dipping oar;
We cannot catch the Boatman's hail,
Nor yet behold the snowy sail.

But, ah! full well we know that they
We loved have surely sailed away;
For pale hands now lie still and cold,
Upon each heaveless breast of mould.

And orbs of light are sightless now,
And chill as marble grows the brow!
Love thrills not through the quiet breast,
Or moves the still limbs from their rest.

But hark! from out the darkness dim,
We hear a loved voice sweetly hymn;
And, lo! the chill mists lift to show
The stream alight with life's pure glow;—

A landscape spread in beauty fair,
And gleaming waves of tinted air,
Pulsing with life's eternal strain,
Baptizing all the heavenly plain.

And, reared in art's exquisite grace,
A grand pavilion marks the place,
Where Perfect Rest her couch hath spread
For those who slumber with the dead.

And white robed forms, upon yon shore,
Await the boat with muffled oar;
And in a starry robe enfold
The wanderer from the earthly mould.

Then Time's dim shores forever fade
In darkness, where the clay is laid;
And holy strains of music rare,
Low swelling, thrill the radiant air.

As up a gleaming pathway bright,
Baptized with beatific light,
They bear the sleeping soul, to rest
In peace, till *thought* shall thrill the breast.

THE SPIRIT MOTHER'S WELCOME.

*Written for the Funeral of an Infant Son of James and Adelle
Snyder, of Courtland.*

Oh! my son, I 've clasped thy treasure,
   Safely in my spirit arms;
Gazed, with love that knows no measure,
   On its little angel charms.

Gently Death's cold hand hath fallen
  On its little fairy form ;
Angels home its soul have callen,
  From life's weary strife and storm.

Earth to earth ;—its dust is sleeping
  Sweetly in this narrow grave,
While your weary eyes are weeping
  For the child you could not save.

But look up:—I tell the story
  Of a beaming land of light,
Where your child, baptized in glory,
  Dwells amid the angels bright.

Yes, look up—I still repeat it—
  Dry your tears, and weep no more ;
But go forth, with joy, to meet it,
  On the radiant spirit shore.

Thus an angel's soul hath spoken,
  This the greeting that it sends :—
"Death no earthly tie hath broken,
  Only made us spirit friends !"

FAREWELL.

Written for the Funeral of Mantie Provin, of Cannon.

Farewell! form of mortal clay,
Hidden in the dust away;
Sunk within the silent tomb,
Mingling with its solemn gloom.

Thou wilt never more rejoice,
With the spring-tide's vernal voice;
Nor earth's grander summer see,
Nor the autumn's loaded tree.

Thou wilt heed no wintry blast,
When the tempest rideth past;
Though it shakes earth's sounding shore,
It can break thy sleep no more.

Farewell! oh! thou crumbling clay,
Hidden from our sight away;
Free from struggling thou wilt sleep,
And I know we should not weep.

But the friend we loved so well,
Whither hath *she* gone to dwell?
Surely *she* can never sleep
In this grave so dank and deep!

Her frail body we have laid
In the tomb that ye have made;
But we know *that* is not *her*,
But the garment that she wore.

Let us lift our tear-dimmed eyes,
From the graves that round us rise;
Far away from death and pain,
Let us seek our loved again.

Let us seek her in the land
Where the white-robed angels stand;
And, amid the throngs of light,
Crowned, our Mantie meets our sight.

While our tears are falling fast,
That her earthly life is past,
She, amid the shining throng,
Sings Life's everlasting song.

Gaze upon her sleeping clay,
Beautiful in its decay,
Where the smile of holy love
Settled as she went above;—

And a radiance that lies
Ever in the angels' eyes,
Flashed and fastened on her face
As she went to take her place.

And dry up your falling tears
For her blighted earthly years;
Love is still her destiny
In the great eternity.

SHE HATH ENTERED REST.

Written for the Funeral of Mrs. Mary Whitney, of Cannon.

The curtains of night were folded round
  My home 'neath the forest trees.
When into my ears there came a sound,
  Like a sighing summer breeze.
Gentle and slow, thrilling, yet low,
  It stole to my being's core,
And angel feet I heard come and go,
  Through the portals of my door.

Those angel forms that gleam like a star,
  In my humble cottage home,
Why have they wandered from realms afar?
  What speak they to spirits lone?
An angel band, from Summer Land,
  That spreadeth beyond the tomb,
A blessing have brought in each white hand,
  For the soul that sitteth in gloom!

Touched with a silvery wand of light,
  My freed spirit went its way,
And stood with this aged form in sight,
  Coffined as you see to day;
Wasted and worn, tattered and torn,
  By the weary march and strife;
On, yea, on to the grave it was borne,
  On, onward, and out of life.

Sadly I gazed on the wreck I saw,
  And wept for the fate of man;
But an angel unfolded the law
  That Infinite Love had planned:—
Youth, life, and love are given above,
  To those who have passed the stream;
I saw *her* then 'mid the risen move,
  And I *know* it was not a dream.

All, one by one, the loved of her youth,
  To the silent grave went down;
Alike, manhood's pride or childhood's truth,
  The fetters of death had bound.
Her heart grew chill while waiting still
  The boat with the muffled oar;
To bear her to the Beautiful Hills,
  Of the blessed Spirit shore.

She struggled long with the monster form
   That was gnawing at her breast;
Oh! fierce was the strife and wild the storm-
   But now she hath entered rest.
In the dawning grey, she passed away,
   To yon glory-beaming land;
And angels sang,—not a feeble lay,—
   But a swelling anthem grand!

" Oh! the winds breathe soft, the skies are bright,
   And flowers are ever abloom,
In the land beyond death's starless night
   In the land where is no tomb.
There buried bliss, lost happiness,
   Is found by the heart grief-pained;
And the soul forgets its long distress
   In joy of treasures regained."

This was the story bright angels told,
   As tranced they bore me away,
And placed me beside this aged mould,
   That is crumbling to decay.
Oh! spirits bright, from lands of light,
   There is one great boon I crave;
That I ever live, like her, the right,
   And triumph over the grave.

IMMORTAL LIFE.

*Written for the Funeral of an Infant Daughter of Amos and
Libbie Christman, of Cannon.*

I saw a bud of immortal life,
   Enfolded in loving arms;   [strife,
But angels swept down, through the world's wild
   And bore it from life's alarms.

Bore it away to a temple vast,
   In the land where souls abide;
The Jordan of death by the babe was passed,
   Without a fear of its tide.

Where the little one dwells no pain hath part,
   No anguish of heart or brow;
No sorrow or strife makes the sad tears start;
   It dwelleth in beauty now.

Oh! that the world, with its weak, dim eyes,
   Adaze with an earthly dream,
Could gaze on the beautiful hills that rise
   Just over the silent stream;—

Methinks that lips would forget to breathe
   A false and envenomed breath;
Or ever a brow with scorpions wreathe,
   To sting loving hearts to death.

For, there, every foot is moving swift,
   To guide some wanderer right;
And every arm is outstretched to lift,
   Souls from darkling error's night.

Hail! beautiful soul! that from this form
   The angels have borne away;
I give thee greeting.   Beyond death's storm
   Thou hast safely passed for aye.

Yes, hail! life germ that sped from this clay
   We place in the silent grave;
We shall meet thee again some future day:
   Life's banners forever wave.

NEVER DIE.

*Written for the Funeral of Mrs. Erastus Edwards, of Follett's
Mills.*

From an earthly home, a beautiful form
   Has passed in the morning of life,
Death folded her in its bosom of storm,
   And swept her away in its strife.

How strangely it seems to move where she moved,
    To gaze on the works of her hand;
To look on the husband and child so loved,
    And also the early home band.

This is the story we briefly may tell,
    As we follow her coffined bier:
" None knew but to love her," won by the spell
    Of her truth and virtue while here.

But while we so loved her, the robes she wore
    Of womanly beauty and grace,
She folded around her, and crossed to that shore
    Whare waveth the banner of peace.

Dear Addie: we call for thee over the hills,
    And over the valleys of earth;
Away, over oceans, lakes, rivers, and rills,
    And up where the starlight hath birth.

The suffering hearts of thy loved ones cry out,
    " Oh! where hath the wanderer gone?"
The hills and woodlands re-echo the shout,
    That dies in the valleys along.

But tones we seek are not heard in the rush
    Of echoes abroad in the land;
To death God hath given the power to hush
    Each pulse by the touch of his hand.

Then, mourners, creep back from the silent grave,
  To the home where her *works* abound;
Bow your heads low, that affliction's black waves
  So madly may trample you down!

Nay, nay; when twilight is gloaming the land,
  And starlight is born in the sky,
The Beautiful One beside you will stand,
  And sing to your souls "Never die."

Nay, nay; when morning awakens in pride,
  And sentinel stars bid good-bye,
Methinks, 'neath the suntide, thy beautiful bride
  Still sings to thy heart, "Never die."

Young husband, bowed down with this weight of
  Oh! lift up your tear-ladened eyes;   [grief,
This beautiful truth must bring you relief,
  The soul and its love never dies.

Forever and aye, beyond the dark tomb,
  Her pathway in beauty will lie;
A white robed angel, dispelling your gloom,
  As ever she sings "Never die."

Mourners, shrink not from the gathering graves,
  That everywhere meet your sad eyes;
'T is God's great blessing, death's outgoing waves,
  That bear us where love never dies.

THE STRAYING CHILD.

*Written for the Funeral of Willis, infant Son of Doritha and
Melville Hill.*

At the twilight hour, a beautiful band,
From the starry realms of the spirit land,
Stood by the couch of a suffering child,
And its spirit form from the clay beguiled.

Oh! 't was a pleasant thing, that childlike form,
Amid the drifting clouds of life's wild storm;
But Death, with his strange wierd fingers, hath stole,
The record of life from the clayey scroll.

The beautiful head, and the brow so fair,
With its curling wealth of sunny brown hair;
A cherub's bright form in the grave is laid,
But *Willie* away to the skies hath strayed.

There is nothing can tempt his feet to roam
From the charming scenes of his spirit home;
Where cherubs of light are his playmate band,
And harmonies swell from cathedrals grand.

His path by a meandering stream is laid,
Where gay song birds trill in each sunny glade;
And he shouts with glee as he gathers flowers,
Abloom by his path in God's own bowers.

But, often indeed, though his heart is glad,
He will turn to loved ones lonely and sad;
You may almost hear his pattering feet,
And feel his caress on each tear-stained cheek.

You have wept sad tears for the straying child,
That angels away from the earth beguiled;
But his flying footsteps have gained the track,
I know, by their light, he can oft come back.

And those footprints shall be like burnished gold,
When the mournful years of this life are told;
And with throbbing heart you will count them o'er,
As you wander off to the spirit shore.

And when clasped for aye is the truant child,
On the seagirt shores of yon spirit isle;
You will thank the Great God with every breath,
That he gave to the earth the angel Death!

THE BEAUTIFUL IMMORTALS.

Oh! beautiful Immortals stand,
Beside each hearth through all the land;
They move where hosts do congregate,
And on the lonely *orphan* wait.

White hands we deemed in death were still,
Are waving now from Life's high hill;
And voices, hushed by death's control,
Are speaking truths to every soul.

They are not lost, those loved ones dear,
They are not lost—they gather near;
And robed in white, unseen they roam,
Close by our side, within our home!

At twilight's hush they gather round,
And oh! we feel 'tis holy ground,
Where angels' feet we know do tread,
Where earthly forms sleep with the dead.

Their hands within our own are laid,
Their bright locks o'er our own have strayed;
Their lips upon our cheeks we've felt,
And sorrows in their presence melt.

The night comes on with silent tread,
And folds dark curtains round our bed;
But still those angel forms are near,
And in our *dreams* their songs we hear.

In dreams we clasp each blessed hand,
And wander through a sunny land,
Where dark despairing casts no gloom,
Or fair forms hide within the tomb.

Our feet with theirs walk life's glad way,
Where shadows never cloud the day;
And hard indeed it seems to wake,
Where time's dark surges wildly break.

They are *not dead*, and in God's time
We meet them in a seraph clime,
Where waves of error cease to roll,
And *truth* illumines all the soul.

MISCELLANEOUS
POEMS.

.

MISCELLANEOUS POEMS.

MY PROMISED LAND.

The Promised Land! the Promised Land!
To thee outstretched is every hand.
In fancy still the yearning soul,
Wraps some far land in gleaming gold;
Where skies are brighter, fields more green,
Than in the "Father Land" are seen.

Look at yon emigrant, who drains
His little purse of hoarded gains;
Through hunger, cold, and want, he wades,
But still his bright dream never fades;
There is a "Canaan" in the west,
Than his dear "Father Land" more blest.

The young man binds his sandals on,
And, ere we know, his feet have gone;
Gone over prairies broad and green,
Seeking the Eden of his dream—
The teeming fields, where his own hand
Shall make a second "Father Land."

Each maiden, in her bridal veil,
Lives o'er again the oft-told tale ;
Her head in loving freedom pressed,
Upon a stalwart manly breast ;
Her dream atint with rosy light,
Puts "Father Land" far out of sight.

The last farewell is said, and now,
The western sunlight on her brow,
At first her fancy sweetly weaves,
A vine-clad porch and drooping eaves,
And *then* a stately mansion grand,
Surpassing all in "Father Land."

'T was thus my parents' eager feet,
Went forth *their* promised land to seek,
When I was but a "wee sma' girl,"
In pinafores and flaxen curl ;
And to old Skaneatlas' shore,
Their straying feet went back no more.

And where found *they* the favored spot,
On which to rear the settler's cot,
And emulate, in years of pride,
Their father's ancient "Ingleside" ?
They found it where the "Queen of States"
Wears, meek, her diadem of lakes.

I love her stately forest trees,
Her dark pines, waving in the breeze,
Her running streams, and hills, and dales,
Clustered like scenes in fairy tales;
Her beetling cliffs sublime and grand,
As aught we saw in "Father Land."

I love her undulating plains,
Rich with the wealth of fruits and grains,
Her deep-laid mines' exhaustless store,
Her many hundred miles of shore,
Her open prairies, free and grand,
Unlike our broken "Father Land."

If God, in some convulsive rift,
Should set our little State adrift,
And on the wild chaotic tide
No sister State rode at her side;
Still self-sustaining she would stand,
Despite the lack of "Father Land."

Her salt, her plaster, and her pines,
Her copper, coal, and iron mines;
Her thousand fields of fruits and grains,
Her cattle, on her hills and plains;
Her fish, and wool, and willing *hands*,
Would make her still the Queen of Lands.

Let *others* wander where they will,
Unsatisfied and restless still,
Seeking their Promised Land away,
Towards the rising, or setting day;
But, till the stars eclipse the sun,
I wear *thy colors*, Michigan.

AUTUMNAL MUSINGS.

Only a few short months agone,
   I wandered in the woody dell,
When early spring was coming on,
   And the breezes had a perfumed smell;—
A fragrance caught from early flowers
That bloomed within its primal bowers.—

The tiny leaflets on the trees,
   Were robed in downy soft green hues,
And here and there were busy bees,
   Sipping the honey-laden dews;
And warblers sang a blithesome song
Through all the balmy spring day long.

But when sweet spring had passed away,
   And lengthened summer sunlight fell,
For hours, in one broad sheeted blaze,
   On the sequestered woodland dell;
While trees assumed a darker green,
Birds sat hushed in their leafy sheen.

But when the blazing orb of day,
   Sank beneath the horizon's rim,
Each tuneful throat poured forth its lay,
   To God—a pleasant evening hymn.
Oh! I have learned, from birds and flowers,
To give to God the evening hours!

Soft breezes rise, and die, and swell,
   When night shades gather o'er the land;
Nature takes on a dreamy spell,
   Swaying hearts with a magic wand.
Passions pause; in the still twilight,
Our spirits own the Infinite.

Oh! I have sat for hours and mused,
   When lengthening shadows crept amain,
And silently the evening dews
   Were sprinkling o'er the grassy plain;
And, one by one, the stars grew bright,
Crowning with gems the brow of night.

And I have dreamed the zephyr's sigh,
  Breathing low, in the still twilight,
Was angels' whispers wafted by,
  On viewless pinions of the night;
And I've seemed drawn from earth away,
Through the gates of eternal day.

Drawn to walk with the blessed throng,
  That somehow ever seem so near,
Though long ago their earthly song,
  Grew strangely hushed upon the ear.
Drawn to walk with angels of love,
Holy ones in the home above.

Then haste ye on, ye fleeting hours,
  With vanished spring and summer sun,
Retracing paths to sonthern bowers,
  When all his northern race is run;
For on thy wings, oh! time, I fly,
To my home in the azure sky.

Yes, the sweet spring, with garlands crowned,
  Clothed with bright tints, the leafless trees;
Here lie her honors on the ground,
  Or, crisp and sere, float on the breeze.
All nature wears a dress of dun,
And sad winds sing a requiem.

List to the dirge of the dying year,
   Passing away, coming and gone;
Beauty laid on a dusky bier;
  . One glad strain, then a solemn song
Hushed in the roaring tempest's blast;—
Lo! in coming, the year has passed.

And thus it is with human life,
   Passing away ere well begun;
While we are arming for the strife,
   Lo the battle of life is done;—
And upon time's resistless tide,
Into the arms of death we ride.

HOPE.

God set thee like a gleaming bow,
To light man's pathway here below.
And when the world the darkest seems,
Thou cheerest with thy brightest beams.

If adverse storms and tempests rise,
And darken all our mental skies,
Ere grim despair can seize the heart,
Thy radiance bids the gloom depart.

Too many times man's truest friends
Are only kept for direst ends,
And cast from him with heedless guile,
When fortunes in his pathway smile.

So, when his bark on pleasant seas,
Moves smoothly onward with the breeze;
Thy starry light he scarcely heeds,
He only seeks thee in his needs.

But, unlike other friends, at last
Thy rays gleam over all unasked;
Folding the soul in holy light,
Even in death's last fearful night.

A DREAM.

I dreamed a dream, a glorious dream,
  Of a temple high and grand,
It stood on the banks of a flowing stream,
  In a bright and sunny land.

I dreamed on still, of gay birds that trill,
  Their strange harmonic notes,
Till the air with melody 's a thrill,
  And e'en to the earth it floats.

I dreamed on still, of evergreen hills,
    And the plains that spread away,
Gem'd here and there with glenting rills,
    That down to the river stray.

My dream grew sweet, for I thought my feet
    Were privileged to walk that way,
And over the river I went to meet
    The friends of another day.

I crossed the tide, by an angel's side,
    And stood on that shining shore ;—
Then I saw what opened my blind eyes wide,
    Mighty truths, not seen before.

Their footsteps stray down a shining way,
    Who 've passed to a higher life,
But their souls came on that strange dream day,
    Covered over with sin and strife.

They took them in, amid song and din,
    Into the temple grand,
Both angel and mortal, e'en truth and sin,
    That day in the spirit land.

The maiden fair, with disheveled hair,
    And heart so sadly broken,
Who of *all* the wide world's *scorn* had a share,
    But not one loving token.

The drunkard's face, with its dark disgrace,
　　I saw its bloated loathing;
And there, too, the poor beggar had a place,
　　Despite his tattered clothing!

The murderer came, while the lurid flame
　　Burned hot in his sunken eye;
His *mother* was there, and her sacred name,
　　Drew his footsteps to the sky!

The orphan child, that was frozen while
　　The Christmas peals rang out,　　　　[aisle,
While *millionnaire* churchman walked costly
　　And plenty was all about!

There sin and shame, of every name,
　　Came gliding in together;
I could not stay with such gathering shame,
　　I, oh! not I! no, never!

I turned away, but a voice said "stay,"
　　And I raised my eyes to see;
'T was my angel mother who spoke that day,
　　As she reached white hands to me!

We crossed the floor to the open door,
　　That angel mother and I;
That mother I had lost so long before,
　　In the grave they laid her by!

And there I saw the Divine Love Law,
   Engraved on the temple's dome,—
" 'T is ignorance only that makes the flaw,
   When men from the right way roam!

Blessed are they who will work and pray,
   Till every soul shall be pure,
Teaching in beauty, a far ' better way,'
   Thus making salvation sure."

Oh! then, I cried, away with false pride;
   Assist me to know the right;
That the erring one I may safely guide,
   From sin's overwhelming night!

Then Mother came, God bless her dear name,
   And gave me a conquerer's wand,
And bade me go forth over hill and plain,
   To save the weary earth land.

I saw that throng, with a joyful song,
   Pass out from the temple grand;   [strong,
Their dark robes fell off, and the weak grew
   That day in the spirit land.

I turned once more from yon shining shore,
   Its temple and angel band;
And stood in this sad world of sin and gore,
   And waved that conquering wand.

Strange to behold were the faces old,
　　Alight with a youthful gleam,
When I said their loved were not dead and cold,
　　I had seen them in my dream.

I tell them all of the templed hall,
　　That stands on a shining shore;
Where crime-stained souls hear the angels call,
　　And go and sin never more.

Some frown awhile, then a sunny smile .
　　Illumines each visage grim;
And old earth forgets its criminal guile,
　　As it sings redemption's hymn.

The. angel band in the temple grand,
　　That stands on a shining shore,
Have wrought out this work with a magic wand,
　　True knowledge for evermore.

There's many a heart whose pulses start,
　　And many a hand grows strong,
And many an earth-soul hath a part,
　　In the overthrowing of wrong.

The march of years, and the dream of tears,
　　With us all will soon be o'er;　　　　[fears
Oh! then how sweet to stand where grief and
　　Are banished for evermore.

Where joy-bells grand, rung by angel hands,
　Peal out from the temple's dome,
Gather, gather them in from out all lands,
　God calleth his people home.

———

MAGGIE'S SPEECH; OR TRUTH AND FALSEHOOD.

Many years ago, on a bright summer day,
Three beautiful maidens went wandering away;
And close by the river's brink, 'neath the green shade,
Many hours together the little ones played.

Far out in the rushing stream's billowy breast,
A huge boulder lifted its bare rocky crest;
And with many a scrambling rush with the tide,
The youngest girl reached it and climbed its steep side.

And then calling back to the two in the stream,
Her voice sounding sweet as the tones of a dream,—
" 'T is a beautiful place, and a pleasant day,
What a pity there's no one to preach or pray.

If I were a man," and her lips firmly pressed,
Told plainly the feelings that throbbed in her breast,
" Oh ! *if I were a man*," now her voice rang clear,
" I would utter great truths that the world might
    hear."

" Oh ! sister," they called back, "just *play* you're a
    man,
And let the old rock be your lecturer's stand,
The sky is the temple's dome over your head,
And yon thundercloud's voice its bell peal," they
    said.

" The gathering waters that look in your face,
Will answer to you in the audience place ;
And the music of waves poured freely along,
Will stand for the orchestra, organ, and song."

So beautiful Maggie, with uplifted head,
Her tiny arms over the river waves spread ;
And feet firmly planted where tides never reach,
Declaimed, for the ages, her first " maiden speech."

" Flow on, gleaming river, and bear on thy tide,
The truth that I utter, to lands far and wide ;
Go tell it where stars shed their beauty at night,
Go tell it mid tropics, where sun rays gleam bright ;

Go tell it where ocean waves dash on the shore,
Or where, down the mountain side, fierce torrents
    pour ;
Go tell it, ye winds, to the children of men,
The dwellers in city, or hamlet, or glen ;
Go whisper it, angels, by pillows of snow,
Where maiden cheeks nestle with innocent glow ;
Great God, bear it home to the aged and youth,
That Falsehood is robed in the garments of Truth !"

And then, with gleaming eyes lifted on high,
She said, " a bright angel, who dwells in the sky,
Tells me, when this world in creation was young,
And grand anthems to God the morning stars sung,
That Truth and her opposite, Falsehood. were seen,
By celestials astray mid its bowers of green ;

Truth walked 'mong the flowers in sandals of light,
With a girdle of stars and pure robes of white ;
Men saw her and loved her, and often would bless,
Not Truth, for Truth's sake, but her beautiful dress !
While Falsehood, the vile hag, in unseemly gear,
Was spurned from their dwellings in loathing and
    fear !

Many years the green earth sped on its glad way,
In its circling flight round the great orb of day,

And ever in sunlight, and ever in shade,
Truth scattered her blessings where men's homes
      were made ;
While Falsehood stalked harmless, her garments so
      vile,
Were known, soon as seen, by the veriest child.
Suspicion and Slander, her broodlings of hell,
Were harmless to work out their purposes fell.

One day, when a summer sun rode in the sky,
And soft southern breezes went whispering by,
And silver clouds sailed in the ether above,
A convoy of angel ships, freighted with love,
Bearing down to the earth their traffic of peace,
Their clearance port Aden, consignment the East.—
Amid the glad beauty of earth, air, and wave,
Truth and Falsehood went down to a river to bathe.

And Truth, with her pure heart unconscious of guile,
Laid down her fair robes, with an innocent smile ;
While old 'haggie' Falsehood, concealing a frown,
Cast off in grim silence her old tattered gown.
Both entered the gleaming tide, Truth giving heed
Alone to the song waves that oceanward speed,
While Falsehood soliloquised thus, as I ken,
' I am cast out of heaven and spurned of all men ;
My garments betray me, wherever I stay,
But " Ye Gods, I'll yet bring the nations to bay," '

For, just then, her eyes wandering off to the shore,
She espied the pure garments that Truth ever wore;
And, gliding away with a serpent-like stealth,
In the mantle of Truth she wrapt her vile self,
Then shouting defiance, she fled from the shore,
While Truth, scorning garments that Falsehood once
 wore,
With flying feet sped on the fugitive's track,
Crying, 'Falsehood, come give me my starry robes
 back.'

And forth from each hamlet that lay on their route,
Where pursued and pursuer sped with a shout;
Men roused by their clamor, turned back, and in ruth,
Exclaimed to each other, 'there goes *naked* Truth!'
And all over the wide world, ever since then,
You hear of the '*naked truth*' spoken by men.

But lo! over earth-homes a deep'ning shade falls,
Distrust and suspicion the weary heart palls;
The fairest fames wither where scandals are rife,
And loves, broken-hearted, are wrecked in the strife.
Falsehood lurks strangely in the hearts of the brave
And often we find the betrayer betrayed!
The nations are sitting in sorrow and gloom,
For human trust shattered, sleeps low in the
 tomb!

Naked Truth, naked Truth, oh ! sadly I ken,
That *seeming*, not *real*, is the favored of men;
For Falsehood is pampered in palace and cot,
While Truth wanders lonely, deserted, forgot.
But speed ye, bright waters, and sing to each shore,
The reign of base Falsehood shall shortly be o'er;
The hour comes apace, mid suffering and ruth,
When men seek again for the Truth—*naked* Truth !"

The maiden's feet splashed in the wave's gleaming
    breast,
And away wandered she at play with the rest;
But little thought she, in some far future time,
A stranger would gather her speech into rhyme !

Years have passed on their pathway of shadow and
    gleam,
And a staid matron now is the maid of the stream;
But out into other years, trust me, will reach,
The *pathos* and *truth* of our Maggie's first speech !

MY MOTHER'S GRAVE.

Long years ago, when twilight dim,
Closed all the gloaming landscape in,
I stood beside the mound of earth,
Heaved in my spirit's wildest dearth;
Hiding a mother's treasured form,
Alike from sunlight and from storm.

My limbs were weary, feet were sore,
For many miles I'd wandered o'er,
To reach and lay my aching head,
On her last damp, dark, lonely bed;
And feel, mid all my woe, so blest,
Thus near her pulseless heart to rest.

Then wildly, from the low, damp clod,
My spirit called to her and God,
Praying through all the long, dark hours,
That God would call me to His bowers,
And let my throbbing temples rest
Forever on my mother's breast.

No voice or token reached me there,
To stay my heart's wild wailing prayer,
'Till cold faint gleams along the sky,
Warned me the day god's feet were nigh.
Then, with my heart o'ercharged with pain,
I wandered to the world again.

But in that hour of wild despair,
God and his angels heard my prayer;
And, though my ling'ring feet yet tread,
The path that leads down to the dead,
Yet oft my throbbing temples rest
Upon an angel mother's breast.

And my torn heart grows strong to bear
The trials counted to my share;
While o'er my brow I often feel
Her soft white fingers gently steal;
And know, whatever may betide,
She walks an angel by my side!

MAN'S PRE-EMINENCE.

A FRAGMENT.

Man holds a place pre-eminent
  To all created things,
That sport the wave, or tread the earth,
  Or float on downy wings.

While wisdom points with gleaming hand,
  To justice and the right,
And turns our feet from every wrong,
  To keep our spirits bright.

VISIBLE FOOTPRINTS OF DEITY.

Go, skeptic, from thy narrow room,
To muse beneath the sky's broad dome,
And let pure floods of nature roll
Their truthful lessons on thy soul,

Pray tell me how yon orb of day
Pursues, unchanged, its pathless way;
Or, how yon brilliant worlds of light,
E'er decked the sable brow of night;—
If there is not a God supreme,—
Naught, naught, save chance's bewildered dream?

Go, gaze on yonder mountain high,
Whose top is towering to the sky,
Where everlasting fields of snow,
Resist the sun god's fiercest glow,
And say, does not its awful nod
Proclaim to you a living God?

Go, perch thee on yon craggy steep,
And view the yawning chasm deep,
Where not a ray of heaven's light
E'er yet illumed its gloomy night;
Where dashing torrents make their way,
Through dismal rifts, in search of day;—
Then tell what power it was that tore
That gap within the mountain's core?

Go gaze adown yon vast abyss,
And hear the seething torrents hiss,
Where subterranean thunders roar,
And desolating fire-floods pour;
Go, learn what mighty force must hurl
That burning lava o'er the world,
Then say, speaks not the crater's flood
The awful majesty of God?

Go, list yon mighty river's song,
As roll its gleaming waves along,
Now gliding still, now dancing light,
Now rushing with the torrent's might;
And oh! to you methinks 't will say,
" God gave me birth and marked my way."

Go, learn how mighty cities fell,
When earthquakes rang their funeral knell;
Or furious whirlwinds hurled their powers
Against their stately domes and towers;
Then humbly bow, and own that God,
Who makes earth tremble with a nod.

Go, watch yon proudly swelling sail,
As it careers with pleasant gale;
Then look again, with eager eye,
When waves are running mountains high;

And from dark clouds the lightnings flash,
And thunders break with awful crash,
While winds in wild, fierce fury sweep
The angry bosom of the deep;
Then say, what keeps that little band,
If 't is not God's Almighty hand?

The tempest-burdened cloud he speeds
The rushing winds His winged steeds;
At His command the lightnings leap,
The thunders break, the whirlwinds sweep.

But turn we from such scenes of power,
To spend a passing transient hour,
In analyzing things that still
Require Omnipresential will.

Behold the sap that upward flows,
By means of which the verdure grows,
Bedecking earth with shrubs and flowers,
Watered with dews and gentle showers;
Then say, if chance is the great cause,
How deals it with those minute laws?

Go thou, with nicest eye, and scan
That strange phenomenon of man;
Tell how his sinews all are strung,
And bones so nicely wrought and hung;

Then tell what power it is that gives
That inward principle that lives ;
For thought, methinks, could never spring
From chance, that blind and *thoughtless thing.*

If with this frame the soul must die,
Then tell me why, oh ! tell me *why,*
Within this heart there burns a fire,
That speaks of something nobler, higher,
Than this frail tenement of clay,
That soon must droop and fade away ?

Why yearn we for a loftier flight,
To purer, brighter worlds of light ?
Why dream we of the hour, when free,
Our home shall be eternity ?
Why born within our souls the cry,
That we may never gratify,
For knowledge of the powers that bind
The universe, and govern mind ?

And why that pleasing, treasured theme,
On which we love to muse and dream,
When friends we love have passed away :
Say why so sweet the thought that they
Like watchful spirits, guard our way ?

And when our path seems lone and drear,
And troubles camp around us here,
And earthly friends desert their post,
And all our brightest dreams are lost,
Why, in that hour of direst pain,
Do *dead friends* seem to live again—
A loving *presence* on time's shore,
Where we walk lonely never more—
If there is not a God divine,
In whose eternity we shine,
Triumphant in the hour of death,
Breathing anew life's genial breath?

Skeptic, in oblivion deep,
Oh! let thy doubts henceforward sleep!
And, with adoring mind, I pray,
Acknowledge God, whose mighty sway
Rolls world on worlds, through yonder blue,
And draws our spirits upward too!

———

LINES

WRITTEN IN A STRANGE LADY'S ALBUM.

Lady, if you are pretty now,
I'd like to kiss your snowy brow;
And, in these few lines sing your praise,
Wish happiness to crown your days.

But should you prove an ugly elf,
Oh! then I'd wish to hate myself.
So I will call this rhyming dust,
Stirred by praise or shy distrust.

BEAUTY'S DEVOTEE

———

SING OF HEAVEN.

Oh! sing to me of heaven,
　When a darkness gathers dense,
Upon my earthly vision,
　Ere my spirit goeth hence.

Oh! sing to me of heaven,
　It will gather bright ones round,
To waft my spirit upward,
　As my body sinketh down.

Oh! sing to me of heaven,
　And of life, and love, and light,
To cheer me through the darkness
　Of death's strange, lonely night.

Oh! sing ye still of heaven,
   When a calm unearthly rest
Has gathered o'er my features,
   And my soul is with the blest.

Oh! sing ye still of heaven,
   For my spirit yet may hear;
And ye may aid its progress,
   With your songs of holy cheer.

For, as from earth forever,
   My frail spirit wings its way,
I oft may pause and listen,
   To the strains of those who stay.

Oh! sing ye oft of heaven,
   And of God who rules by love,
Around your earthly firesides,
   And I'll join you from above.

I'll sing to you of heaven,
   When I dwell amid the blest;
I'll sing of all its beauty,
   And its calm eternal rest.

Just fold your hands and listen,
   When the twilight gathers round,
I know you'll hear the angels,
   And my song with theirs shall sound!

How very near together
    The Heavens and earth appear;
When men sing holy refrains,
    And the angels stoop to hear.

Oh! sing a song of heaven,
    It will lift your thoughts above
The passions of the earth life,
    With its swelling strains of love.

———

STRUGGLE ON.

He who is foremost in the van,
Sees first the long sought "Promised Land;"
Who plants his flag on freedom's soil,
Is first exempt from slavish toil.

Who bursts the chains of binding power.
Knows then the sweets of freedom's hour;
Who stands upon a mountain's height,
Sees first the coming morning's light.

Who longs to *live* beyond earth's day,
And walks with angels on the way,
Learns thus the mighty truth that he
Is heir to immortality!

Do friends turn blindly from your path,
And curse you in their holy wrath?
Are all your worldly treasures gone?
For truth's own sake still struggle on.

Others have fought the deadly fight
Of truth, against oppressive might;
The Press its massive power hath shown,
Though Faust was called the "Devil's own."

The lurid lightning chained, to-day
The calm behests of man obey,
Outstrips the sun in rapid race,
And turns to naught all time and space.

It anchors England at our shore,
Despite old ocean's sullen roar;
Yet, in past days, how scoffs and sneers
Fell on the brave projector's ears.

Kings, priests and potentates this hour
Both praise and use the lightning's power;
But *some* remember curses loud,
When Franklin tapped the thunder cloud.

And when a Morse presumed to tell
That lightning might be made to spell,
Men turned with scorn from his wild scheme,
And called it a " Fanatic's dream !"

So, when a Fulton launched his boat,
And steam was fairly set afloat,
It broke his heart and purse, they tell,
And lost him many friends as well.

But now the whistle sounds his name
From every flying railway train;
And all our lakes and oceans float,
" *Success* to Robert Fulton's boat."

The Genoese, who opened wide
This new world o'er the western tide,
Reaped only chains and sad disgrace,
Yet how he blessed the human race.

So everywhere, in every age,
As all may learn from hist'ry's page,
Men crucify great souls who try
To bless the world before they die.

Yet God hath made the heart so brave,
That *some* can conquer e'en the grave;
For future years can give their all,
And drink the hemlock or the gall.

And God hath granted the free soul
The power to watch the ages roll;
Not one has toiled for human needs,
But sees his work when it succeeds.

Then struggle on for truth and right,
Your body may be out of sight
When that great truth its place shall find,
But it shall surely bless mankind.

———

LINES

ADDRESSED TO ADDIE HAYNES, ON HER MARRIAGE
WITH F. M'COLLIER.

Dearest Addie, gentle maiden,
   Flaxen haired and earnest eyed;
Going forward to love's Eden,
   Walking by a manly side.—
May thy earthly journey never
   Lead thee down to sorrow's vale;
But repeat ye, each to other,
   Day by day, love's oft told tale.

Oh! full well I know that, drifting
  Round the earthly homes of all,
Many wrecks of joys are lifting
  Shattered fronts, our hearts to pall;
But, in thy united striving,
  In the battle heat of life,
Each for *each*, oh! still be striving,
  Loving *husband*, loving wife.

Let the earnest wifely duties,
  That thy new relations bring,
Only give thee added beauties,
  And a sweeter song to sing.
May the hearth light that ye kindle,
  Mid the homes of men to-day,
Be it e'er so small an ingle,
  Make earth brighter for its ray.

Farewell, maidenhood and girlhood,
  With thy careless dreamy hours;
Some would tell us there is no good,
  Save within thy sunny bowers.
Gentle Addie, fair-haired maiden,
  Folded close in wedded arms,
Angels bless thee, may love's Eden,
  Trance thee ever with its charms.

SCOTIA'S SOUVENIR TO THE BRIDE.

ADDRESSED TO ADDIE ON THE SAME OCCASION.—(IN-
SPIRATIONAL.)

And sa', sweet lass, a bonny bride,
  I saw ye, yester e'enin',
Wi' a braw laddie by your side,
  And smiles your e'e agleamin'.

Sae ga' the gait ye started on,
  Wi' ye'r ain chosen laddie,
And may na' sorrow fa' upon,
  Your head, sweet bonny Addie.

Oh! may yoursel' be always gay,
  Nor heart, nor hand grow weary,
In sawin' seeds of love each day,
  To reap them wi' your dearie.

May bli'some weanies come to glad
  Your hearts beside the ingle;
For sooth that housie maun be sad
  Where kimmer can na' mingle.

May leesome grace fa' to your share,
  Wi' worldly gear a plenty;
And when death craikens in your **ear,**
  May lo'in' friends a' tent ye.

And bonny angels reach their han's
    Across the silent gloamin',
To lift your feet upo' the stran's,
    Were ye'll nae mair gae roamin'.

———

BURNS' SPIRIT DOON.

Ye banks and braes o' bonnie Doon,
    I wad na' ye should bloom less fair;
I wad na' that ye little birds
    Should sing ane song o' wofu' care.
My heart's a' strang, ye little birds,
    That warble i' the sunny burn,
I ha' nae mair o' parted joys,
    Departed never to return.

Yonder I mourned the hawthorn's bloom,
    The primrose and the daffodil;
For me the summer a' had gloom,
    The brae wept sad aboon the rill.
The daisy and the heather grew,
    The gaily flowering, flashy broom;
.But she wha was my heart's dear light,
    Was sleeping in the silent tomb!

I cou' na' bear the lint white's sang,
  It ga' my heart fu' muckle pain;
But when death brake o' life the band,
  I found my highland lass again.
I may na' tell ye o' the flowers
  That bloom along the paths we walk;
No a' the joys o' holy hours,
  'T wad seem to ye uncanny talk.

But blithely roll, thou bonnie Doon,
  Gae dance thy runnin' way alang;
Auld Scotia's flowers send forth perfume,
  And birdies sing ye'r sweetest sang.
There is no selfish grief o' mine,
  I wad na' care to you impart;
But sing o' her wha is enshrined
  Upo' the tablets o' my heart.

And sometimes, too, auld floods o' Doon,
  I wad that ye should wake the glade,
Wi' something that would mind ye'r lads
  O' Burns, wha sany within ye'r shade.
I wad na' be a ghaist for aught,
  I'd only ha' ye tent o' me;
And find o' wit I splored ye out,
  A swatch to meke ye better be.

THE SONG OF GOD.

A FRAGMENT.

This beautiful world, with its bending skies,
Where the stars look out like angel eyes;
The blade of grass, with its emerald hue,
The blooming shrub, and the drop of dew;
The loftiest tree, and the lowest clod—
Are singing forever the Song of God!

Then arise, my soul, with all thy powers,
Converse with God in the star-lit hours;
Wherever thy wandering feet may stray,
Where forests wave or waters play,
In the twilight's gloom or noontide's blaze,
Sing ye, forever, His sacred praise!

IDLEWILD.

Idlewild! Idlewild!
Beautiful foster child
Of a bright spirit flown,
To the soul's summer gone.
None will thy name repeat,
Save in memoria sweet,
Of the world's gifted child,
Gone from thee, Idlewild.

Never my feet have strayed
Into thy quiet shade;
Where the sun's golden gleam
Brought summer's leafy sheen;
And nature's rhymeless song,
Warbled by birds along;
Where dwelt proud genius' child,
Willis, of Idlewild!

But I have dreamed of thee,
Dreamed what ye ought to be,
When I have bathed in light
Flashed from his pen point bright,
Gleaming along the lines
Of his smooth flowing lines,
And I knew sunset smiled
Sweetly on Idlewild.

I knew a murm'ring sound,
That not a hum had drowned,
Of running waters came,
Falling around the fane,
Where his pure spirit knelt,
Where nature's beauties dwelt,
From their rough form beguiled,
Into his Idlewild.

I knew his home must take,
Beauties his soul could wake;
Nature through art be seen,
Art but to crown her queen.
Nature, with sandaled feet,
Walked through thy calm retreat,
And, from its windows smiled,
Beautiful Idlewild.

He who had wandered long,
Mid lands of art and song;
Strayed classic shades among,
Where ancient bards had sung;
And his whole soul baptized,
Neath the Italian skies,
Knew how to make thee smile,
Secluded Idlewild.

But now his song is hushed,
Neath sods his heart is crushed;
Cold is his hand, and still,
That once our hearts could thrill;
Thy sylvan shades are mute,
Broken the silver lute,
That once a world beguiled
With strains from Idlewild

And, like an echo, strays,
Each strain from other days,
As his white garments gleam
Ever across the stream.
No other song shall swell;
We have his last farewell;
Death hath his feet beguiled
From his loved Idlewild.

Now ye charm angels' ears,
Through the immortal years;
While mortals mourn for thee,
Not thy bright destiny,
Thy joy amid the blest,
Nor thy eternal rest.
We mourn our *loss* awhile,
Sweet Bard of Idlewild!

OH! MAKE ME A GRAVE.

Oh! make me a grave in some shady dell,
  When life from this form shall have fled;
But let no vain column be raised to tell,
  Where sleepeth the unconscious dead.

Oh! make me a grave, when silent I lie,
　That will call no stranger that way;
And lay me to rest 'neath the twilight sky
　Of a calmly departing day.

Oh! make me a grave, when calmly I sleep,
　The sleep that hath never a dream,
Where sun rays blend soft with shadows that creep,
　At twilight, o'er woodland and stream.

Oh! make me a grave where the moonbeams rest,
　When nature hath sunk to repose;
A sheen of light on the clods that are pressed
　O'er a heart, and its youthful woes.

Oh! make me a grave where the streamlet plays,
　And the soft breezes gently sigh;
And the brow of night, with star-fires ablaze,
　Shall light my path on through the sky.

Oh! make me a grave where my friends may bend
　To muse with affection and love;
When far out mid sun-worlds my path shall tend,
　With the blessed who throng above.

Oh! such be the grave of the lonely one,
　Just a lonely grave may it be;
Sought only, when this poor life shall be **done,**
　By the *few* who *knew* and *loved* me.

ADVICE.

Never wed a dreaming poet,
Or an artist, if you know it;
  Men who fold their hearts in shrouds,
  Woven mid the tinted clouds,
  Know not how the hands must toil,
  In the dark, unseemly soil;
How wearily the feet must tread,
That bring the idling dreamer bread.

Ideal women, robed in white,
Girdled in morning's roseate light,
  " Eyes that quench the diamond's glow,"
  " Pearls," instead of teeth, you know;
  Feet that only deign to " trip,"
  " Rosebud " mouth and " ruby " lip;
Tapering fingers bound with rings,
Angels, not girls, the poet sings.

Woman, made all of gossamer,
That just the slightest breath can stir
  Into motions full of grace,
  In this dull world have no place;
  And what seems so is a cheat,
  Mocking the pursuer's feet.
Time's fingers rub the tinsel off,
Then poet's lips will only scoff.

He who lives in the ideal,
Uses still, but scorns, the real.
  Deities, the poet sings,
  Never scorch their tissue wings,
  By the cook-stove's ardent glow,
  Broiling beefsteak here below.
Yet those who wield the brush or **pen,**
In dining rooms are only *men.*

Again, I tell you, wed no dreamer,
He will eat your toil-won dinner,
  And go back amid the stars,
  Solaced by perfumed cigars ;
  And, as solids cannot fly,
  Useful labors neath *him* lie.
Some one's lily hands must soil
With needful unaspiring toil.

Somebody very sordid seems
To him who only lives in dreams.
  Girls, take up the warp of life
  With one who 's equal to the strife ;
  One who weaves his beauty dream
  Into something felt and seen ;
One who only dreams to labor
For the good of friend or neighbor.

ON, ON.

How many the mementoes
　　We see along our road,
That earth is not our dwelling place,
　　Our spirit's firm abode.

In childhood our days seem long,
　　The hours are moving slow;
In our maturer years they fly,
　　And how we scarcely know.

The present joy we heed not,
　　But to the future look;
Expecting something better still
　　Within its unsealed book.

Science ope's its golden gates
　　To the aspiring mind;
We heed not that we have attained,
　　There 's something *new* to find.

Ever thus the spirit pants,
　　Still reaching on ahead;
And never pauses in the race
　　Till we are with the dead.

What we shall do beyond the vale
　Is more than I can tell;
But, judging from our earthly course,
　Where hopes forever swell,

We shall not cease to reach ahead,
　To that beyond our ken;
For ever onward seems the course
　Of the free souls of men.

———

CARRIE, THOU ART REMEMBERED.

Dearest one, thou art remembered,
　Mid the cares around me here;
And right gladly art thou numbered
　With the friends I hold most dear.

And, may, I receive a token,
　Sometimes, that you ne'er forget
That the stranger spell was broken,
　Or that we have ever met.

Silently this missive paper
　Speeds it to its destined place,
And, for want of something better,
　Of kind thoughts the only trace.

I recall the depot station
  In that little dreary place;
Somewhere, in this Yankee nation,
  Where I last beheld your face.

Sitting at the open window
  Of the hot and dusty car;
I beheld you swallowed into
  All that crowd of noise and jar.

Then away the train went sweeping,
  With its stranger throng and me,
And a shadow slowly creeping,
  Wrapped me in its density.

All alone! the words came leaping
  From my tortured heart of pain;
All alone! in solemn keeping
  With my whole life's sad refrain.

Oh! I know that we shall never
  Meet again this side the tomb;
But your image, shrined forever
  In my heart, dispels its gloom.

Think of me when joy is round you,
  And your heart beats light and glad;
Think of me when sorrow's night dew
  Falling, makes your spirit sad.

And our friendship, be it ever
   Pure as angels' love might be;
Shedding radiance forever
   Over all our destiny.

LINES

ADDRESSED TO THE CHILDREN OF THE OAKFIELD PROGRESSIVE LYCEUM, MARCH 30TH, 1867.

Children, these many days we've met,
   An earnest, thoughtful band;
Repeating lessons for us set,
Guiding our inexperienced feet
   To knowledge's temple grand.

We've gazed upon creation's page,
   With earnest, anxious eye;
And like philosopher or sage,
We've boldly asked the green earth's age,
   And paused for a reply.

Then all the starry hosts that speed
   Along the pathless blue,
The deep laid rocks, the barren glebe,
The ocean wave, the sunny mead,
   Have gladly answered you.

Brave ones, this world by God was made,
   These countless years away ;
Its corner-stone in Him is laid,
Therefore its rays can never fade,
   But grow to "perfect day."

We asked of God,—and all the flowers
   Made us this sweet reply,
" By babbling brooks, in sunny hours,
With swelling buds, mid breezy bowers,
   God's love can never die ! "

Thus, with a firm yet modest hand,
   We knocked at science's door,
And wisdom ope'd its portals grand,
And bade us welcome to the band
   That seek for hidden lore.

But, children, when your days are told,
   That to the earth are lent,
Remember, gathered mines of gold,
Nor all the wealth the Indies hold,
   Could change a life misspent.

Then in each being's early morn,
   Be this the constant prayer :
" Let high resolves in me be born "—
And, in temptation's wildest storm,
   You shall be conqueror.

INDEPENDENCE DAY.

READ AT A GROVE MEETING, JULY 4TH, 1855.

Hark! away over hill and woodland
The boom of cannon comes,
And you hear on every hand
The sound of fife and drums.
What means the cannon's deafening **roar**,
The spirit stirring lay?
Why, 'tis to tell from shore to shore—
'Tis Independence Day!

Our country's flag floats on the breeze,
Those Stars and Stripes we cheer,
While underneath these spreading **trees**
Freemen are gathered here,
To celebrate the boon we found
O'er eighty years away:
When freemen cast from them the crown
On Independence Day.

Then was the hurrying to and fro,
And faces pale with fear;
As mothers bade their darlings go,
While brushing back each tear.
The cannon's roar meant something **then**,
When booming far away—
For, it was mowing down *true men*—
That Independence Day.

Up through many a contest hot
Our cause has struggled on,
And crowning Peace has been our lot
These many years agone.
In peace the gathering crowds now meet
Where the free oaks do sway,
To celebrate our Nation's Fate—
Great Independence Day.

Long may assembled millions keep
This day to honor men
Who dared the cry of " Treason " meet,
For sake of progress then.
'Twas independence that they sought
From foreign tyrants' sway;
And that great boon, their blood hath bought
Since Independence Day.

May we, their children keep the trust
Our fathers handed down.
May not progression's plow-share rust
Inactive in the ground.
May sons and daughters of the brave—
As each year rolls away,
Speak, and *act*, for bond and slave—
On Independence Day.

If tyrants strive to curb free thought
Or brand with "treason's" cry—
Let them a freeman's hate be taught
Now, as in days gone by.
May noble children of brave sires
Sweep the last chain away;
Then with pure flame burn Freedom's fires
On Independence Day.

———

A FRAGMENT.

Great truths are written on the sand,
But ere waves desecrate their pages;
Effect, the Stereotyper grand,
Steps forth, and with recording hand
Preserves them for the Ages.

———

TO MRS. L. A. MORSE.

The Widow's mite: God bless, God bless,
The Widow and her mite.
You freely gave your little all,
And wept because it was so small:
God bless the Widow's mite.

MY HOME.

Oh! my earthly home is an humble cot,
   A cottage of low degree,
But flowers make fragrant the quiet spot,
   And trees nod their heads to me.
And every nook is hallowed ground
   In that humble home to me,
For there my earthly treasures are found
   As I count them, One, Two, Three.

And many come back from the other land
   Beyond Death's silent river,
Oh, I feel the touch of each angel hand
   Is blessing me forever.
And too, what if my earthly home is mean?
   I live in a palace rare
There is many a child of wealth I ween
   Would give much the like to share.

You smile; but I mean the Palace of Love
   That a heart hath reared for me;
Its cool colonnades, with roof flowers above,
   Is that heart's great trust in me.
And I seek their shade when the sun's fierce glow,
   Is consuming all outside;
I turn to that roof when the wild winds blow,
   O'er sorrow's engulphing tide.

And it never fails me, never; oh! no!
    It gleams in the sun's bright light;
And as firmly stands, when the tempests blow
    In the wildest, darkest night.
There's a gallery, too, within our home,
    Where memory's pictures smile;
And all are there, not a loved one is gone,
    That hath blessed our way awhile.

And our home is rich with exotics rare,
    That bloom near the zone of the heart;
And there's many a shady pathway where
    We two walk, never apart.
Oh! then tell me no more I live in a cot,
    That is poor, and mean, and low;
When love's rarest flowers bloom on the spot,
    All wealth a heart can bestow.

GOOD TEMPLARS.

One morning this old world awoke,
And saw amid its battle smoke,
A gleaming banner, pure and white,
Fronting the early morning light.
That gleaming banner, free and grand,
Is waving o'er a temperance band,

That everywhere are gathering force,
Like ocean in its tidal course.
   King Alcohol we fight to-day,
Though all his minions stand at bay,
And never will our hosts disband,
Till we have conquered all the land.

   Look at the army of the king,
And list the songs his cohorts sing;
They bear the stamp of slave and vassal,
And all their songs are rant and wassail;
Singing still, they reel and stutter,
Or sleep like swine along the gutter!

   The "new recruit" 's a "jolly fellow,"
Who only gets a "little mellow."
Years go by in drunken rattle,
And now he stands in front of battle;
Poor battered object to behold,
With bleary eyes, where *loves* grow cold!
Oh! let us leave him there to rot,
It would not pay to save the sot!

   But, hark! I hear a mother's prayer,
For her *lost son*, float on the air;
No pathos hath mere *words* to tell
What feelings in *her* bosom swell!

His heart is fire, his blear eyes dim,
King Alcohol hath conquered him,
Or else her pleading wail would stay
His footsteps on the downward way.

Templars, bring back that mother's joy,
Save, oh! save her treasured boy;
Save, despite his manhood's treason,
Alcohol hath drowned his reason!

While I gaze, before him kneeling,
Comes another, love appealing,
And a group of children gather
Round that kneeling wife and mother!
Mayhap, no word her lips are speaking,
But his heart her eyes are seeking.

"Oh! for days of sunny gladness,
Ere this blighting, drunken madness;
When a fair-haired, gentle maiden,
Walked beside thee to love's Eden.
Oh! for sake of bonnie bright eyes,
That came to make our Paradise,
Cease to serve the great destroyer,
Break the chains of the annoyer,
And come back to be the glad life
Of thy mother, child, and lone wife.

Be the staff that is sustaining
A father's years, so few remaining;
Shoulder to shoulder with thy brother,
Conquer life's great boon together;
While thy sister's pure caresses
Tell thee she is proud who blesses."

Thus her breaking heart is wailing,
But her prayer is unavailing;
For, behold! the demon, shaking
His clenched hands above her quaking,
Tramples her beneath his treading,
Turns child-love to horrid dreading,
And, with a God-denying breath,
Goes out to quaff his moral death.

Oh! Templars, for the sake of those
Who suffer more than mortal woes,
Unfurl your banner 'neath the sky
And fight till Alcohol shall die.
Fight, till the serpent of the still
Uncoils from man's subjected will.
Charge on the strongholds where they turn
Bread into *fires* that seethe and burn.
Charge on their outposts at the bar,
Break every vile decanter there;
Down with all license for the sale
Of all the wares of Bacchanal.

Then tattered garb and bloated face,
And breaking hearts and vile disgrace;
Then manhood's wreck and orphans' tears,
And squandered wealth and blighted years;
The hangman's rope, and prison bars,
And paupers' graves beneath the stars,
Will find no place, but evermore
Shall swell the Templar's grand *encore*;
Sounding along the land and sea,
Triune, Faith, Hope, and Charity!

And, as for him who sells the stuff,
I find no language strong enough
To draw his portrait; low and mean—
The creature's self needs to be seen!

"Respectable," I hear you say!
Great God! *that man* who steals away
The loving husband from the wife,
Robs *him* of everything, e'en life;
Steals from the child its father's arms,
Dragged downward by most devilish charms;
Steals mind, and love, and wealth away,
And makes man demon by his sway!
The highway robber is a *king*,
Beside the mean ignoble *thing*.

Brave souls, true-hearted everywhere,
Come up and help us in this war;
Till all may walk the paths of earth,
Uncursed by this wild maddening dearth!

FIRESIDE MUSINGS, Jan. 11th, 1864.

Winter comes on with dreary tread,
   Around our cottage home;
The hours, like mourners for the dead,
   Wail as they march along.

The mystic life of plant and tree
   Has hid itself away;
No flowers allure the little bee
   From its warm hive to stray.

The waves, a little time gone by,
   Gleamed with a sunny hue,
Now heave beneath a lowering sky
   Chilled to a steady blue.

The trees with bare and frozen limbs,
   The northern blast resist;
In southern lands the wild bird hymns,
   His song is hushed in this.

No leafy bowers entice the birds
 From those soft summer skies;
And kindly *acts* and loving words
 Must make *our* paradise.

Only a little time agone,
 We wandered forth with joy;
Each path we took detained us long,
 The fields gave sweet employ.

But now we through the windows gaze
 On fields enwrapped in snow;
King Frost subdues Sol's feeble rays,
 Within, the hearth fires glow.

The trees afford our heads no shade,
 No flowers our feet attract;
No babbling brook sings through the glade,
 Now, life and death compact.

But round our cottage fireside, warm,
 We gather from our toil;
Close sheltered from the sleety storm,
 Old winter's self we foil.

Sweet Flora, straying from our land,
 With all her buds and flowers;
Will come again, with offerings grand,
 To deck the vernal hours.

But, while she wanders from our shore,
  Lo ! by the " ingle's " blaze,
My muse shall weave her rhymic store
  Of song, for sunny days.

She 'll sing us something sweet to know,
  To make our home seem bright,
While fierce outside the wild winds blow,
  This weird and wintry night.

My cottage home beneath the trees,
  That wave their brawny arms,
In song or wail to wind or breeze,
  Oh ! say what are thy charms?

I fain would sing of running streams,
  Of mountains stern and high ;
Of manhood's hopes or childhood's dreams,
  Or friends to death gone by.

And oh ! full well methinks I'd sing
  Of all that patriot band,
That to the breeze our banners fling,
  And fight for our dear land.

Full well I'd sing of bleeding hearts,
  Pierced doubly through and through !
In many cots, their hidden smarts,
  Our God alone may view.

Yet none of these my muse employs,
  This weird and wintry night;
But fireside scenes, domestic joys,
  For these she curbs her flight.

I look around my humble home,
  And question what I see,
To tempt her near my cot to roam,
  And weave a rhyme for me!

Lo! through affection's gleaming tear,
  A noble form I see;
The locks upon his brow grow sere,
  Long years he's lived for me.

Yes, long ago, in his young pride,
  His manhood's pride, I ken,
He took me for his "bonnie" bride;
  He loves me now as then.

His brawny breast and strong kind arms,
  Have been my shield for years;
He's sheltered me from life's alarms,
  And stayed grief's bitter tears.

These years gone by he's gathered us,
  My little ones and me,
To his great heart of love and trust,
  And bade us happy be.

Some of our band have passed from earth,
  Beyond the gates of even;
But e'en of death we lose the dearth,—
  For we shall meet in heaven.

We gather closer in our love,
  We who remain together;
And in our sorrows look above,
  Trusting to God forever.

Oh! none may sing the joys of *home*,
  With adequate refrain;
How wand'rers wheresoe'er they roam,
  Long to return again.

Oh! how the firelight on the hearth,
  The lamplight through the pane,
Will reach them through the world's chill dearth,
  Calling them home again!

"You're almost home!" The bounding heart
  Stands still with crowding bliss,
And holy teardrops freely start,
  At one such hail as this.

"I'm almost home,"—and dying eyes
  Flash up with mystic light,
And white hands fold, as to the skies,
  Our loved pass out of sight.

Home! 'tis a blessed word I know,
  I've conned it o'er and o'er,
Where sweet peace sits, though wild winds blow
  Right fiercely past the door.

My cottage home beneath the trees,
  I love thee when the sun
Looks downward, and a southern breeze
  Drifts flowers and song birds home.

But, now I think of it, I find
  Whatever may betide,
I hold thee dearer when, love twined,
  We near the ingle side.

A TRIBUTE OF LOVE.

At twilight I sat in my own quiet room,
While night hung her curtains of gold and of gloom,
And gazed on the fast fading beams of the day,
Till I seemed in a land away, far away.

I stood on the banks of a beautiful stream,
In a world as bright as a midsummer dream,
Where the changeful hues in the sky o'er my head,
Rivalled aught of splendor in tales I had read.

A musical sound, like the rushing of wings,
And a strain, like the song the seraphim sings,
Subdued in my bosom the tumults of life,
And drew me away from the world and its strife.

Then a voice I had heard mid the world's wild din,
Called forth from a palace, " Come in, come in."
I stood by the voice, 't was an angel, I knew,
And he bade me return with a message for you.

And *this* was the story the bright angel told,
Up yon, in his palace of opal and gold,
Where mountains upheave in the distance away,
And ocean waves roll to the gateway of day.

" My father, dear father, full many a time,
I've striven to send you a greeting in rhyme,
And as often have failed for want of a way,
To write in earth language my one little lay;
But now I'm controlling a hand just as true
As the steel of the patriot soldier in blue;   [will,
And backward, oh! backward my thoughts flow at
To the home where you dwell, oh! the house on the hill.

Your form is bowed down with the weight of much
    care,
And silvery threads streak the dark of your hair;

I know you are weary, as onward you tread
The pathway that leads to the 'house of the dead.'
And darkness hangs thickly your vision around,
Because in *your* home I am not to be found.
But father, dear father, I dwell when I will,
In the home where you dwell, oh! the house on the hill.

My mother dear, neath the oak tree's shade,
In a southern land, my grave is made,
Where the glinting waves go rushing by,
Beneath the sun of a tropic sky!
Where flowers, to you exotics rare,
Bud and bloom in the genial air;
Where the southern birds of gorgeous wing,
From out my leafy tombstone sing.
Away, from the land of blood and strife,
My spirit passed to the grander life.
I sat in the shade by yonder tide,
Dreaming of you on the old hill side,
When the bullet sought life's hidden springs,
Bowing my head to the King of Kings;
But in the march of the coming years,
Oh! stay the tide of your falling tears,
For in and out of the open door,
Coming and going for evermore,
Dear Mother, remember, I dwell when I will,
In the home where you dwell, oh! the house on the
hill.

My brother, you and I were boys,
  But a little while ago,
Together gathering up life's joys,
  With its little crumbs of woe.

Now I stand upon the mountains
  That o'ertop the hills of earth,
While *you* dwell beside the fountains
  That beneath my feet have birth.

And once again we will be boys,
  When the Boatman bears you o'er,
Gathering up unfading joys,
  On life's better, hither shore.

But know, while you tarry, I walk when I will,
In the paths where you walk, by the house on the hill.

My sisters, you ask *where* my home may be,
Mid the rolling waves of eternity's sea;
And I turn my eyes from the quiet nook,
The house on the hill, and the mill by the brook,
And gaze through the golden gateway of rest,
Far outward and on to the land of the blest;
Its highlands and vales, its skies calm and clear,
Lying far, far away, and yet, oh! how near!
Then I turn and reply, I dwell when I will,
In the home where you dwell, oh! the house on the hill.

Yet a home I have, 't is a mansion grand,
A palace of light in the bright spirit land;
From distant hills, where the white marbles glow,
I have sought rare blocks, and with chisel and blow,
Outwrought with my hand, for my palace fair,
An image of each in the old home there.
Yes, dears, we are here, all of us, you see,
And those who are living in heaven with me!
So, whether in palace or home by the mill,
I live with the loved, oh! the house on the hill!

THE WANDERER.

Tell me, ye southern winds,
  That breathe around my home,
Where in the sunny southern climes
  My brother wanders lone?

What strange mysterious spell
  Has fallen round his lot,
That those he used to love so well
  Are seemingly forgot?

Has Mississippi's wave
  Sundered affection's tie?
Is southern soil my brother's grave?
  Tell me, ye winds, I cry.

Thus my sad heart doth wail,
  Unto the wailing wind;
It whistles past, but tells no tale
  Of him I wish to find.

Sometimes my moan is hushed,
  Into my heart alone;
I sit and think of songs that gushed
  In days that are agone.

Of days the muses swept,
  With thrilling hand, thy lyre;
My brother, love had never slept
  Beneath their sacred fire!

Brother, your silence seems
  So like the grave or death,
Asleep I dream "uncanny" dreams,
  Awake I seem bereft.

We gather round the hearth,
  And talk and talk of thee;
I write, but still there is the dearth
  No word comes back to me.

Go forth, ye breezes, go,
   And whisper in his ear,
That in the land of sun and snow,
   His memory still is dear.

Our teardrops, as they fall,
   Freeze round each troubled heart;
No sun but love can pierce the pall,
   And melt their ice apart.

Oh! brother, for the love
   Of her who went away,
To walk the sacred courts above,
   Oh! so many a day—

Let each of us she bore,
   Cling closer. side by side,
Till we shall reach the shining shore,
   Beyond death's darkling tide.

In far-off Michigan,
   By Bostwick's gleaming strand,
My unaccustomed lyre I've strung,
   And struck with trembling hand.

Like bulbul's whistle sad,
   When broodlings are away,
One answering note—her song grows glad,
   Where leafy tree tops sway.

May Nina's song be heard,
 A low and plaintive cry;
And, may her brother's heart be stirred
 To make a quick reply.

————

EOLINE.

CHAPTER I.

" Life is a dreary waste, at most,
Where one by one our hopes are lost,
 And teardrops fall in vain;
They have no power to fertilize,
The arid waste that round us lies,
 Though they are poured like rain!

Far in the distant past are set,
The bright hours I would fain forget;
 Their memory brings distress.
Followed so soon by bitter scenes,
They only mingle in my dreams,
 Without the power to bless."

Thus plaintively Eoline sang,
And through her sad lay sometimes rang,
　A wail-cry of despair;
Too well I knew a phantom train
Of shattered hopes brought back the pain,
　It broke her heart to bear.

And who was Eoline? you ask,
Imposing thus the mournful task,
　To write life's histories;
Revealing to the world at last,
Causes that oft our high hopes blast,
　The soul's deep mysteries.

—o—

CHAPTER II.

Men tell us earth's a " vale of tears,"
Walled in with human doubts and fears,
　And *far* o'erhead a God,
Whose providence, along the years,
Bears off our friends on pall-clad biers,
　And hides them 'neath the clod!

Well *somewhere* in this world of woe,
Eoline's sunny ringlets glow,
   And her glad song-trills gush;
And *there* the darkling shadows grow,
That bid her bounding feet move slow,
   And all her bright hopes crush.

And *somewhere*, too, a mother lies,
With folded hands and death-glazed eyes,
   Where churchyard shadows creep;
But well I know, with heart of love,
That mother watches from above,
   Her daughter's weary feet.

You may not call *her* Eoline,
That strangely saddened child of thine
   Another name may bear;
But still within my verse outlined,
Or painted closer still, you find
   Her soul-life written there.

Perhaps *your* child has passed away
From the glad realms of light and day,
   Down to the grave's dark gloom;
Or, yielding to the hollow play
Of custom's false and heartless sway,
   Dwells in a living tomb.

It matters not; the song I sing,
Through all the castes of life will ring,
   A warning voice of truth;
And to the startled conscience bring,
How teachers plant a poisoned sting
   In the pure heart of youth.

Most every one, upon whose head,
A score of years their hours have shed,
   Has felt the withering blight,
That falls around the spirit's way.
When superstition's fearful sway
   Obscures the soul's true light.

Oh! foolish man!   Why seek to find
Distorted thoughts to feed the mind,
   Perverting God's plain truth?
Why seek for demons through the land,
And dive to hell for spirits damned,
   To fright the souls of youth?

Why give untoward *fancy* wings,
And label " carnal " all bright things
   That earthly pathways fill?
Why blot the love-light from our sky,
To give us past mythology,
   As God's most holy will?

Why wonder at the fearful sight,
When law of "like producing like,"
   Stands gazing in your face?
Or walks the earth with baleful eye,
Or hides in prison walls to die,
   A criminal past all grace?

How can you turn with placid air,
From brick walls on the hill-top there,
   Where howling madmen rave?
Was 't God or *man* who swept the light
Of reason from its altar bright,
   In a false scheme to "save"?

God never made a criminal soul,
And never will while ages roll;
   His labor is divine.
Sin is perverted mental thought,
Into eternal action wrought,
   Men *make* and call it "crime."

Fables of demons fierce and fell,
And lurid sulphur-flames of hell,
   Begin the fearful task;
And, darker still, a God of ire,
Than demons, in his wrath, more dire,
   Completes the work at last.

What wonder that the world is rife
With jealousies and bitter strife,
   With scandal, hate, and lies?
What wonder fierce embattled hosts
Are poured where human hopes are lost,
   Beneath smoke-hidden skies?

Oh! give young children beauty scenes,
Take all dark visions from their dreams,
   Oh! strew their way with flowers;
And in their souls will spring no wrong,
No deadly passions, fierce and strong,
   To blight life's later hours.

" 'T is ignorance that multiplies
The wrong" that in our pathway lies,
   And not a power unseen.
When this great truth is recognized,
And by mankind is justly prized,
   The world will stand redeemed

—o—

Chapter III.

In vine-embowered cottage neat,
A calm and beautiful retreat,
   Wrapped in with sun and shade,
By waves that rolled, a river bright,
Eoline's eyes first saw the light,
   And there her young feet strayed.

Where lofty trees bent o'er the stream,
And flecked its sunny banks of green,
   With everchanging shade;
Their glint leaves moving in the air,
A rhythmic strain of music rare,
   By wind-harps ever played.

Where violets, with modest grace,
Looked in the fair child's winsome face,
   From every quiet nook;
And gayer flowers, with brighter hues,
Sprinkled with morning's pearly dews,
   Her childish fancy took.

All nature had a voice to greet,
With welcome strains, her straying feet,
   And charm her listening ears;
The torrent's or the tempest's chime,
Gave to her soul, crescendo-lined,
   The music of the spheres.

Oh! how she loved the rocky crest
Of highlands, lifted in the west,
    Where gleamed the morn's first ray;
And rolling down the craggy steep,
Night shadows moved in slow retreat,
    Before the god of day.

Entranced, for hours she watched the clouds,
That wrapped the mountain top like shrouds,
    Hiding the tempest's feet;
Where lightnings ran with serpent grace,
And jarring thunders rang a base,
    To lowland music sweet.

Eoline's summers came and sped,
Her mother sleeping with the dead,
    None cared for the strange child;
Save one fair sister sweet and wise,
And one brave brother, in whose eyes
    She said "the angels smiled."

Her father, always sad and grave,
Walked to his toil like patient slave,
    Exact to come and go;
For him, the scenes of life each day,
Moved on the same accustomed way,
    Like ocean's ebb and flow.

His heart lay cold beneath the spot,
Where bloomed the sweet forget-me-not,
   Above his buried wife.
His crushed soul never woke to weep,
He only walked like one asleep,
   Through all his frozen life.

His children watched, mid hopes and fears,
The progress of his blighted years,
   Till life the anchor drew;
And, standing out before the breeze,
Their father's bark, on unknown seas,
   Faded from mortal view.

But, ere he passed from mortal sight,
His shadow fell a chilling blight
   On Eoline's glad way;
For, with a cold and ruthless hand,
He broke affection's sacred band,
   And darkened all life's day.

—o—

CHAPTER IV.

The want of cash! the want of cash!
Hath power our brightest hopes to dash,
   Like leaves cut down by hail;
But when strong hearts and willing hands
Strike out for self, in these broad lands,
   There's scarce such word as "fail."

Then who dare crush affection's bloom,
And bury hearts in misery's tomb,
   Because of yellow dust?
The answer meets me everywhere,
For broken hearts are not so rare;
   "In *gold* men put their trust."

Reader, my pen is not o'er strong,
To write up all of human wrong
   That meets my weary eyes;
For sure, oh! sure, my heart would break,
If in my verse all woe should wake,
   That weeps beneath the skies.

But let me stay that parent's voice,
Who treats with scorn a fair child's choice
   Of heart mate for the years;
For ye are crushing out the light
That made thy child an angel bright,
   Thou'lt find it soon with tears!

Oh ! strange indeed it seems to me,
That those who brave their destiny
   To their own instincts true,
Should fail to recognise the right
Of other hearts to prospects bright,
   That ardent fancy drew.

But so it is.   All through the years,
Sad hearts are sapped by misery's tears
   That flow, and flow, and flow;
Till, like a parchment old and dead,
They only rustle 'neath the tread
   Of scenes that come and go.

And those who are so strangely changed,
By brothers, sisters, are arraigned
   As hard, or cold, or mean;
But, ah ! whose hand the blow hath given,
By which the heart's deep fount was riven,
   That makes them what they seem?

Years passed, and fair young Eoline,
With guileless feet approached the shrine,
   Of pure young womanhood;
And in her soul there sweetly grew
A nobler love than childhood knew,
   Love for young Elinwood.

How strange, that one who loved so well,
Should fail to recognise the spell,
   That bound his winsome one,
Should fail to recognise the smart
That tortured 'her poor bleeding heart,
   When hope's brief race was run.

In vine-clad porch, at eventide,
Lover and loved stood side by side,
   Watching the dew drops grow;
And weaving plans beneath the moon,
Plans to be shattered, oh! so soon,
   By one fell heartless blow.   .

Side by side, in the moonbeams bright,
She in her robes of spotless white,
   The love-light on her face;
He with the wealth of dark brown hair,
With bearded lip and manly air,
   A sovereign in his place!

Look at them well, oh! father cold,
And, standing o'er the sacred mould
   Of one as fair as she,
By all thy manhood wrapped in night,
Cast on their loving hearts no blight,
   No stain of misery.

But, ah ! in vain the spirit pleads,
Urging its own diviner needs,
  Before a world-wise soul;
The seething agony that dries
The heart and brain, to careless eyes,
  Is happy self-control.

Young Elinwood had claimed his bride,
And, by a haughty father's pride,
  Been ordered from the door;
And Eoline, stunned by the blow,
With pale lips bade her lover go,
  And see her face no more.

Forth from that moonlit porch, vine clad,
With hope not lost, but heart o'er sad,
  He walked with manly pride;
Eager to win him wealth and fame,
And earn, 'mong men, an honored name,
  And *then* he'd claim his bride.

But Eoline, with scared, pale face,
Sought only for some lonely place
  To hide her misery;
Nor ever dreamed to break the thrall
Of him who cast a blackening pall
  O'er all her destiny

He who had clasped her, when a child,
To his torn heart, with anguish wild,
   Above a pale, dead wife;
Who came to nestle in his arms,
Bringing no wealth but winning charms
   Of her own beauteous life;

That father slept as calm and still
As if his iron hand or will
   Had crushed no heart that night;
Nor deemed that aught save wounded pride
Had either heart a moment tried:
   'T would heal—the wound was light.

—o—

CHAPTER V.

Again, it is a summer night,
And dewdrops gleam like diamonds bright,
   Neath Luna's silver ray,
As up the road, on charger black,
Young Elinwood comes dashing back,
   From gold fields far away.

But 't is not now the peaceful cot,
With vine-clad porch (their trysting spot),
   On which he stops to gaze;
No; 't is a stately mansion grand,
With costly gifts from every land,
   That holds him with amaze.

He knows full well the "old squire's" place,
And hope-light fades from out his face,
   For, at the window, stands
Eoline's form, as still and cold
As parian goddess draped in gold,
   With clasped and lifted hands.

One long, wild, wail-cry of despair
Rang out upon the moon-lit air,
   One gleam of white hands tossed;
And then she vanished from his sight,
Like dreamy vision of the night,
   Lost, lost; forever lost!

What boots it now, that eager strife,
For gold, at peril of his life,
   Peril on land and wave?
Peril by shipwreck on the main,
Or black death on the fever plain,
   ·Where many found a grave.

He shakes his bridle rein on high,
And with a mad light in his eye,
    Shouts like a trumpet blast—
" On, Sultan, on !   We 've rode before,
Where dangers thronged the land and shore,
    This ride shall be our last !

Thou 'st never failed when conquering bays
Flung their green wreaths, in bygone days,
    Upon my fevered brow ;
Thou 'st ever been a faithful friend,
Yes, true and faithful to the end,
    And thou 'lt not fail me now !

When shattered is my earthly goal,
Gone, gone, the well-spring of my soul,
    Unbent life's arching bow ;
And dark lie shadows on my path,
And fortune flings me scorn and wrath,
    Yes, scorn, and wrath, and woe !

Life's day in darkest night is set,
Good Sultan, I would fain forget,
    Away, away, away ;
Bear me with flying feet, brave steed,
Past vine-clad cot and dewy mead,
    From all these scenes away.

Dash on! wild spirits of despair
Shriek round me through the midnight air;
   Dash on! dash on! dash on!
And Eoline, with mocking face,
Eludes me erst, in rapid race,
   Now here, now there, now gone.

Hist! yonder, where the moonbeams creep,
Through mists that rise above the deep,
   Just o'er the cataract's breast,
I see her in her bridal veil,
Crowned with a wreath of moonbeams pale,
   On, Sultan! do your best."

Urged by the cruel spur, the steed
Flies o'er the dew bespangled mead,
   Down to the river's brink,   ·
Swerves for a moment on the shore,
Then leaps where fearful whirlpools roar,
   And horse and rider sink.

—o—

CHAPTER VI.

Woman; strange tangled mystery!
Taught, even at your mother's knee,
  The slave's one word, "obey";
How sad your epic life I sing,
Touching my lyre's deep, tragic string,
  For there its key notes lie.

God gave you, in your natal hour,
A soul endowed with mental power,
  And wants and wishes grand;
But *man* has bade your spirit's play
Yield strict accord to custom's sway,
  And wear a galling band.

Dare never to forget that you
Were born a woman.   Meekly bow
  In abnegation low;
Just with your foot the cradle rock,
And with your fingers darn the sock;
  That is your "*sphere*," you know.

Or if your *husband's* wealth shall place
You in a wax doll's gilded case,
  Why shine, and be content;
Thankful somebody deigns to spare
Yourself from toils that others share,
  In which their lives are spent.

Oh! many times I've paused to tell
The blighting curse where slavery fell,
  Darkening the soul with hates;
When bondsmen toiled beneath the rays
Of tropic suns, that fiercely blaze
  O'er many southern States;

But shrank to speak, for fear of scorn,
The thousand wrongs to *woman* born,
  Of ignorance and pride;
Walked meekly as I could my path,
While outraged nature, in her wrath,
  Strode ever at my side.

But, hark ye, *now* I will not stay
The deep-voiced truths that swell to-day,
  Within my being's core;
That woman's hand, so white and free,
Shall guide her own soul's destiny,
  Now and for evermore.

Toil? Yes! Behold the millions now,
With battered hands and tan-stained brow,
  That toil mid want and tears;
While, from their bitter labors wrung,
A pittance, ofttimes scornful flung,
  But keeps them half their years.

Yes; toil ye well, with *brain* and hand,
But, as ye labor, firm demand
   A recompense requite;
Give to the daughter as the son,
A recompense for labor done;
   This is eternal right.

Man wraps his huge protecting arms
Round woman, and her boasted charms,
   And *lets* her do *his* will!
He legislates for *her* inded,
And keeps her from her soul's great need,
   By his protective skill.

He taxes her and *spends* the tax,
But, should her moral state grow lax,
   And to great crimes e'er lead,
Why then he wisely steps aside,
And *lets* the *hangman's rope* be tied,
   Or *dungeon walls* succeed!

Woman, your hand is needed where
All legislative bodies are,
   For your own soul's behest;
Break open with your own strong hand,
Each man-locked door to knowledge grand,
   And be an honored guest.

Plead not for "Woman's Rights." For shame!
My soul detests the *trickster* name,
  Wherever it is heard.
Just speak for *human* rights and needs,
And gain the cause by noble deeds,
  That noble thoughts have stirred.

Say to the ballot box, "be clean";
And to the judge, unjust or mean,
  " Lay down the *ermine* white."
And to the host on tented field,
"Thy cause unjust full quickly yield,
  This earth shall know but right."

Now man walks sideways to the dome,
Where law upheaves each mighty tome,
  For human woe or weal;
And *policy* constrains his hand,
When revolution stirs the land
  With progress' holy zeal.

In all life's devious paths our feet
Are tripping at the things we meet,
  Because we walk apart;
And vile dependence degradates
Each woman's life, till bitter hates
  Are born within her heart.

And war unfurls his banner red,
And vengeance glowers o'er the dead,
  On every battle field;
While, by the tortured mother's knee,
Wrong sows the seeds of misery,
  That frightful harvests yield.

Man, woman, read the cause of crime,
Writ by the tracing hand of time,
  On earth's historic scroll;
And learn that he who weaves a wrong,
Will find it twisted in a thong
  To scourge his shrinking soul!

Brother, unbar wealth's gleaming doors,
On all earth's many, many shores,
  And give your sister room;
Then aged groom and youthful bride
No more in costly homes will hide,
  This side the silent tomb.

Then breaking hearts no more will wail,
Beneath the sacred bridal veil,
  Or false vows sear the soul;
Then bride and groom shall proudly stand,
Erect and equal, hand in hand,
  An independent whole!

Chapter VII.

The years go by on lagging wings,
And never now Eoline sings;
  Music for her is dead!
She shrinks when glad waves meet her eye,
When star-fires light the midnight sky,
  Or moonlight beauties spread.

A stunning sense of wrong and pain,
Rings ever, like a sad refrain,
  Through all the weary years;
As restlessly, from room to room,
She wanders through her stately home,
  Dry-eyed, in search of *tears*.

Till clasped unto her aching breast,
A tiny infant form is pressed,
  And a weak wail-cry broke
The spell that on her spirits lay,
And bade her life hopes sweetly play,
  As this new joy awoke.

Ah! human lips are all too weak
A mother's holy love to speak,
  Its magnitude of bliss;
Untiring watch, a life-long zeal,
Unfaltering still, in woe or weal,
  Express its mightiness.

But this sweet love oft comes to bless
Our hearts with its great happiness,
    And fill our paths with light;
Then floating upward, while we gaze,
Our longing eyes with tears adaze,
    The " wee one " fades from sight.

But as our·spirits ebb and flow,
T'ward home above, or home below,
    We catch, or lose a star,
That, as we gaze, grows to the form
Of love, engulfed in death's chill storm,
    Shining forever there.

Oh! how our panting spirits tread
The path that leads beyond the dead,
    Out to our heavenly home,
Eager to clasp each darling heart,
Close to our own, where friends ne'er part,
    Nor lonely footsteps roam!

At first, through grief, our tear-dimmed eyes
See only where the stark form lies,
    The cold remains of love;
But ever, in our deep distress,
God's angels move, our souls to bless,
    And draw our thoughts above.

So Eoline, pale mourner, wept,
Above the form that sweetly slept,
  The sleep that knows no waking;
And dark despair his mantle cast,
Around her shrinking form at last,
  And pierced her sad heart, breaking.

That torn heart, sobbing forth its moan,
A dirge in one brief word, " Alone, '
  Alone, oh! God! how wild;
Her pale lips struggling for a prayer,
Her white hands frenzy-clasped in air,
  Poor stricken, stricken child.

Then, through the darkened, sombre **room**,
Draped in its sad funereal gloom,
  A nameless *something* steals;
It wraps the mourner kneeling there,
And lifts the load of dark despair,
  Her anguished spirit feels.

That *something* gentler than the breeze,
That softly breathes mid whispering trees,
  When twilight shadows creep;
Hushes with mystic power to rest,
The wild storm raging in her breast,
  And, voiceless, bids her sleep.

Gaze on that mother, pale and fair,
Sleeping, so sweetly sleeping there,
  By her dead darling now;
His curling locks of sunny light,
Mingling with tresses dark as night,
  That shade the sleeper's brow.

Lo! while I gaze, the darkened room,
With all its sad and sombre gloom,
  Fades from my weary sight;
And grander drapings seem to fold,
The mother and her darling cold,
  Upon a couch of light!

And, moving through the pulsing air,
That throbs with music rich and rare,
  Bright shining hosts appear;
And foremost in that angel band,
I see a form and visage grand,
  Close to that couch draw near.

A holy radiance round him plays,
Divinest pity in his gaze,
  Yet mighty strength of will;
As back he turns the shining host,
And points them to the gleaming coast
  Just o'er death's river still.

And, keyed to music rich and rare,
His voice thrills through the chiming air,
　　And through my being's core,
As, with a cadence sadly sweet,
He bids the hosts, in slow retreat,
　　Stand marshalled on that shore.

He touches now the sleeper's breast,
And, rousing from her dreamless rest,
　　Wide open flash her eyes,
And, with a mother's boundless joy,
She clasps again her angel boy,
　　In strange yet sweet surprise.

Death hath not touched her with his wand,
But, neath the spirit's trancing hand,
　　Her visioned soul is free ;
And all the loved she mourned as dead,
Glide round her with an angel's tread,
　　In holy ecstacy.

For many hours, upon the bed,
Her cold form sleeps beside the dead,
　　While her free footsteps lie
In paths where angels ever glide,
And loved ones walking by her side,
　　Take all her pain away !

And lead her up where gleaming lies
Mount Pisgah, near the eastern skies,
  Revealing far and wide,
The Holy Land, where Jesus bled,
And heavenly plains in beauty spread
  Beyond death's swelling tide!

Judea's highways teem again,
Beneath her feet, with busy men,
  And round its sacred fane,
The devotees. from far-off lands,
To worship, where its temple stands,
  The great Jehovah's name.

Its hills o'erspread with olive trees,
Its vineyards purpling in the breeze
  Low breathing o'er its vales,
Gleamed neath her gaze, as long before
She read in scripture's quaint old lore,
  Its legendary tales.

But, mid the peace that God hath laid,
O'er sloping hill or sunny glade,
  A wail of woe is stirred;
The nabob, in his silken gown,
With sandaled feet, is treading down
  The *common*, toiling herd.

Now, mid the poorest of them all,
A mean clad form, erect and tall,
  Moves with a pitying eye;
And sick, and dying, and the dead,
Throng ever where his *bare* feet **tread,**
  And unrebuked draw nigh.

Woe, hunger, want look in his face,
As here and there, from place to **place,**
  His great heart leads him on,
To heal the frame o'ercharged with **pain,**
Or bid lost hope revive again,
  When love to death hath gone.

Friends throng his way and kiss his **feet,**
Or seek him in the low retreat
  Where he may chance to dwell;
And fawning sycophants cry "Lord,"
And hail him "Master" with accord,
  While fame rings loud her bell.

But now far denser grows the throng,
Like angry waves they rush along,
  And angry voices ring—
"Seize him, the traitor, and the knave;
Wine-bibber, heretic," they rave,
  "Seize, seize the would-be king."

Loud, and more loud, the tumult grows
Till he, the "man of many woes,"
   Is captured, scourged, and bound;
While leper healed, and he once lame,
Join the accuser's loud acclaim,
   And plait with thorns a crown!

Or frame the cross with hellish zeal,
For him who neath its timbers reels,
   Up Calvary's gloomy way;
Or mixes vinegar with gall,
Or shout when madmen loudly call,
   "Come save thyself, we pray."

But, lo! the tread of heavenly hosts
Shake all the land from coast to coast,
   And awful voices wail;
As backward reels the shrinking crowd,
Aghast, beneath the fearful cloud
   That darkens mount and vale.

But still His dying speech, for good,
Rings o'er that guilty multitude,
   To his great instincts true;
His calm, sweet voice pleads once again,—
"Forgive these dazed and blinded men,
   They know not what they do."

The vision faded from her gaze,
While yet Eoline in amaze
    Stood tranced the scene to view.
It passed away, with shuddering might,
And, lo! the world grew into light
    And beauty strange and new.

"And such is man," a sad voice spoke,
"Wearing for aye sin's galling yoke,
    And rending him whose hand,
Despite all suff'ring and tears,
Works out the good of coming years,
    In faith, sublime and grand!

Look! earth has marched the heavenly way,
Since then, full many a sabbath day,
    Towards eternal right;
Still, men enthralled in sin appear,
Where wrong holds court with ghastly fear,
    And sceptred custom's might!

Each era hath its martyr souls,
That crucifixion firmly holds
    Within its cruel arms;
But, lo! the law of recompense,
Clothes them with deathless radiance,
    And high and holy charms.

That draw the eyes of coming men,
And, while they gaze, inspire them
   With an unswerving zeal,
To *live* the life thus typified,
The *thought* for which men fearless died,
   The martyr's great ideal!

Earth's brave ones, with great wealth of soul,
Stand shining marks, to point the goal
   For those who lag behind;
And, firmly chained by sympathy,
To human needs and destiny,
   Lift up the halt and blind.

Clear-eyed, they gaze where shining cause
Walks Godwise; where eternal laws
   Effects from cause increase;
Clair-audient hear the swelling song,
Clair-prescient bid the struggling throng
   Behold the Mount of Peace!

Daughter of earth, this task is thine,—
Go rouse the darkened, stulted mind,
   Waken great thoughts of good;
Go forth in all the spirit's power,
And labor till thy dying hour,
   For brother, sisterhood.

Lo! one by one, no hand to save,
Thy loved have sought the silent grave,
   And through its portals dim,
Have entered on the path that lies
Forever neath soft tinted skies,
   Where joy lips ever hymn.

Adversity great strength hath lent,
As oaks firm stand, by tempests bent;
   And holy ones above
Their guard and watch will ever keep;
Frail child of earth, 'Go feed my sheep
   With strong kind words of love.'

Gird ye with truth's own armor bright,
And speak great words of living might,
   'Gainst every sin and wrong;
And when men cry 'lo! here! lo! there!'
Turn not aside or weakly spare,
   But fight truth's battle strong.

Lo! scoffers in your path will hiss,
False friends betray you with a kiss,
   And calumny will smite;
Fear not, for sailing down the years,
Meet recompense for toil and tears,
   A blessing heaves in sight.

Then gibbet, prison walls, and jail,
The widow's moan, or orphan's wail,
No more will greet the day;
As joy is born of pain and tears,
Earth seeks her glory-beaming years;
Go labor, wait, and pray!"

FINIS.

AGENTS WANTED.

We are engaged in the publication of a series of POPULAR Books and FINE STEEL ENGRAVINGS, which are Sold exclusively by Subscription through canvassing Agents. We give employment to a large number of MEN and WOMEN, and are constantly in want of more.

CLERGYMEN, TEACHERS, DISABLED SOLDIERS, LADIES, and all persons of either sex who are active and intelligent, cannot fail to succeed in this business; it requires but little capital and no risk—the daily sale of a very few copies amounts to a large sum in the course of a year—with energy and perseverence you can make money and in a manner that will contribute to the intellectual and moral elevation of mankind, (we consider every book agent a moral colporteur, going into the highways and byways of the land, and circulating knowledge where it otherwise would not reach), and your own improvement, and thereby educating yourself in that knowledge of the country and of people and things which is acquired only by travelling and observation.

We publish none but first class books, by the *best* authors, consequently they are the books that every intelligent person wants, and is always ready to purchase.

We shall endeavor to be always able to furnish our Agents with something new and desirable that they *can sell.*

We assign every agent exclusive territory of their own selection, (if possible,) and offer the *most liberal* terms.

For circulars, information, etc., address,

S. S. BOYDEN, Publisher,
73 Clark Street,
CHICAGO, ILL.

☞ *Please read the next two pages.*

THE BOOK FOR THE MILLION!

—o—

90,000 COPIES SOLD IN FIVE MONTHS!!

—o—

Life of Abraham Lincoln,

By MRS. P. A. HANAFORD,

Author of "Our Martyred President," "The Young Captain," "Field, Gunboat" Hospital, and Prison," &c., &c.

"THE PEOPLE'S EDITION,"—only Life of Lincoln written by a woman.

Opinions of the Press.

"Mrs. Hanaford wields a vigorous pen, and has the somewhat rare faculty of grouping facts and men, events and measures, into a befitting and effective attitude. Accordingly, in a book of 216 pages she has compressed the most interesting acts, speeches, sentiments and personalities of the late President. The task must have been difficult, but it has been accomplished with a skillful hand. Those who read this book—and it will become one of the most popular that have been written—will find recorded all that is essential or of interest in respect to Mr Lincoln, and the whole set forth in earnest graceful language. It appears to us to be the precise book the great masses want—something interesting and reliable, and at a very low price. It contains a very fine steel engraved likeness of Mr. Lincoln, and also several woood cuts illustrating the earlier and later scenes in which the lamented President passed his life. The style of the volume is neat, the typography handsome, and the paper clear and graceful."—*Boston Post.*

"Mrs. Hanaford has written for the people, and with them the volume will become "a household word." They will show their little children the homes of Lincoln, as they appear successively in its pages. The rickety shanty in Kentucky; the log cabin in the Illinois woods; the comfortable dwelling in Springfield; and lastly, the White House at Washington. These cuts alone, with no printed word of explanation, exhibit a career unparalleled in the history of man; present a summit of sublime grandeur reached by honest effort and steadfastness of purpose."—*Boston Volunteer.*

"For the religious and moral portion of the community, the author has given a most acceptable history; the illustations are numorous and fine, and the entire work is most eminently fitted for family reading. It is not so pretentious as many of its contemporaneous publications, but quite as reliable and pleasing as any of them."—*Chicago Journal.*

"The book has had a sale of 90,000 copies in five months, and is favorably received in all parts of the country. It contains a fine steel engraving of Mr. Lincoln, and many wood cuts. The work has been translated into the German language, by the celebrated Dr. Wurzberger, of New York, and every intelligent German will have a copy."—*Detroit Tribune,and Advertiser.*

'It is so cheap that every family in the land can afford to have a copy."—*Detroit Free Press.*

"It is handsomely illustrated, substantially bound, and is emphatically a book for the people. It is a work that should be in every family, and its great popularity is attested by the fact that over 80,000 copies of it have already been sold."—"*The Daily Citizen,*" *Juckson, Mich.*

"It is beautifully written, and put up in a neat little volume of nearly 250 pages, and its low price brings it within reach of all."—*Racine, Wisconsin, Journal.*

"It is cheap and comprehensive, and will be popular with the 'millions.' "—*Peoria, Illinois, Transcript.*

"It is by far the cheapest, and is one of the best biographies of Lincoln that have been written."—*Chicago Evening Post.*

"It is not burdened with long documentary matter, but contains all the essential and important events in the unparalleled career of the 'Martyred President. The work is having an enormous sale."—*Terre Haute, Ind. Express.*